MHI Copy 3

FM 72-20

DEPARTMENT OF THE ARMY FIELD MANUAL

JUNGLE OPERATIONS

DEPARTMENT OF THE ARMY • JULY 1954

*FM 72-20
DEPARTMENT OF THE ARMY Washington 25, D. C, 12 July 1954
JUNGLE OPERATIONS

Chapter 1. GENERAL CONSIDERA- Paragraphs Page
TIONS 1-8 3
2. OPERATIONS
Section I. General 9, 10 12
II. Effect of jungle on operations._ 11-13 13
III. Factors influencing jungle tactics. 14-17 14
IV. Troop movements and marches. 18-25 15 V. Offensive combat 26-38 31
VI. Defensive combat 39-44 45
VII. Retrograde movements 45, 4G 50
Chapter 3. EMPLOYMENT OF SUPPORTING ARMS
Section I. Infantry 47-51 53
II. Artillery 52-61 61
III. Antiaircraft artillery and naval
gunfire 62, 63 65
IV. Tank unit employment 64—6-6 67
V. Engineers 67-72 69
VI. Close air support 73-75 73
VII. Chemical, biological, and radiological warfare (CBR) 76-81 74
Chapter 4. COMMUNICATION 82-87 80
5. SERVICE AND SUPPLY
Section I. General 88-90 85
II. Medical Service 91-104 89
III. Evacuation 105-107 108

This manual supersedes FM 72-20, 27 October 1944.

Field Manual No. 72-20

CHAPTER 6. UNIT AND INDIVIDUAL Paragraphs Page
TRAINING
Section I. General 108-110 • 110
II. Practical hints for jungle living- 111-118 112
III. Tactical training 119 119
Appendix. REFERENCES 138
INDEX 140

CHAPTER 1 GENERAL CONSIDERATIONS

1. Purpose and Scope

This manual describes the difficulties of military operations in a jungle and explains how they may be overcome. It describes how military units may most easily navigate a jungle, and is designed to amplify accepted tactical doctrine and techniques when applied to jungle operations. It tells how to solve the problems of supply and establishes the methods that must be practiced for individual and group survival.

2. General

a. Military operations in the jungle combine the many types of combat that are considered as special operations. They include combat in dense woods and mountains, night fighting, and river crossings, all under extreme weather conditions. The difficulties of terrain, weather, and visibility complicate the vital problems of command, movement, and supply to the point where normal methods must be modified and specialized equipment employed.

b. The jungle offers so much concealment and limits visibility to such an extent that surprise in the attack and defense may be exploited to an unusual degree. Formations are more compact and are similar to those employed in normal night operations. To maintain direction and control, small columns are

used, almost to the point of actual combat. Movement is restricted, tending to stabilize and to limit objectives.

o. The unhealthful climate and rugged terrain of the jungle may seriously affect the physical and mental condition of a command. To counteract these hazards, men must be in the best possible physical condition and trained in living successfully in the jungle. Men must be trained not to fight the jungle but to make it work for them against the enemy.

d. The need for decentralized control in jungle operations and the extreme importance of small unit action demand the highest development of leadership among all commanders. The development of initiative, boldness, and determination on the part of these commanders and the development of self-reliance on the part of the individual soldier are major training objectives.

3. Terrain and Vegetation

The term "jungle" brings to mind a picture of impenetrable forests filled with animal and insect life, poorly illuminated and forbidding in appearance, but no jungle is insurmountable to a determined military force. The following types of jungle may be encountered:

a. Mangrove. This type is found near the jungle edge or in a beach area." It is characterized by thickly interwoven roots and branches (fig. 1). Coral reef outcroppings and the muddy flooring of areas flooded by the tide make movement exceedingly difficult. The amount of cutting necessary to effect a passage makes normal operational movements impracticable. Observation is restricted to a dis-

Figure 1. Mangrove roots make movement difficult.

tance of 10 to 15 feet. Vehicular movement is impossible until roads have been built. The mud in mangrove areas at times reaches a depth of 4 feet.

    b. Primary Growth. Densely interwoven vines and trees border the inland streams and fill the valleys, imposing the same limitations on movement as the mangrove jungle.

    c. Grass. Further inland, vast areas of grass are frequently encountered. The grass terrain is normally flat or slightly rolling, but sometimes continues into the foothill region. This grass grows from 3 to 9 feet high, and resembles the grasses of temperate zones. The underfooting is fairly firm and quite stable for wheeled and tracked vehicles. Movement on foot in this type vegetation is difficult because of the height of the grass. Lack of visibility makes night operations in grass lands precarious.

    d. Ridge Lines. The terrain encountered on leaving the grass regions of volcanic islands is characterized by high, narrow, steep-sloped ridges of coral or lava. These ridges are often covered by vegetation that does not greatly hinder the movement of military units.

    e. Rain Forest. Rain forest covers more than a third of the jungle area of the world. These jungles have a normal expectancy of 300 to 350 inches of rain each year. The tree trunks grow to a height of 50 to 75 feet, where they branch out into dense interlocking foliage, making a roof which shades the jungle floor and keeps it in constant semidarkness. The floor of this type jungle is covered with a mat of decaying vegetation. The density of trees varies from the widely spaced ones of old forests, to the new forests, dense with secondary growth. The traffic-

ability of rain forests depends primarily on the age of the forest. Observation is good in older forests, being limited only by the lack of adequate light. In new forests, undergrowth frequently limits visibility to a very few feet. The dense matting underfoot gives suitable traction for vehicles and absorbs the sounds of movement.

    . Secondary Groroth Forest. These areas are characterized by tall trees and thick underbrush. The growth may reach a height of 20 feet. Movement in secondary growth forests is as difficult as it is in mangrove forests (fig. 2).

    g. Cultivated Areas. Improved areas under cultivation resemble the improved areas of other parts of the world and present the same military problems.

    4. Weather

In general, jungle weather is hot and humid, and is characterized by sudden changes. Within a short period of time clear hot weather may change to torrential rainfall. With equal suddenness the rain may cease and sunshine on the soaked vegetation will produce the maximum relative humidity. Humidity is constantly high because of the swamps and the shading effect of the vegetation. There is a rainy season during which monsoons prevail. Seasonal changes in weather are noticeable but not pronounced. In tropical mountains the nights are frequently cool.

    5. Military Characteristics of Jungles

    a. The dense jungle undergrowth and its swamps, sharp ridges, and rivers hinder movement. An enemy will take full advantage of these natural ob-

Figure 2. Movement is difficult and dangerous in secondary growth forests.

stacks in planning defensive positions and may be expected to supplement them with man-made obstacles. The attacker usually maneuvers to seize critical terrain features in the enemy rear and thus make his forward positions untenable.

    i. Critical terrain features in the jungle include defiles, trails, high ground, and communication centers. Objectives will be difficult to identify and observe because of the limited visibility.

    c. Routes of communication in the jungle are meager or nonexistent. Good roads seldom exist initially; the trails are narrow and generally poor. Routes of supply must be built and maintained under the most difficult conditions. Supporting weapons are often limited to mortars and recoilless weapons since artillery frequently cannot be moved forward.

    d. The overhead canopy of jungle growth obstructs aerial observation of activity on the ground. Observation from the ground may be limited to as little as 5 yards, making it difficult to select good observation posts. Sites for indirect fire weapons must be carefully selected to provide mask clearance with a minimum cutting of overhead vegetation.

e. Except in the areas covered with grasslands, concealment is always available. Large forces can move without being seen and patrols can pass within a few yards of each other without mutual discovery.

6. Organization

a. Most standard Army units are suitable for extended operations in the jungle. Certain modifications ma\'7d' be necessary, and will consist usually of a reduction in the number of wheeled vehicles with a proportionate increase in the number of tracked or

light maneuverable vehicles, and an increase in the number of service elements. Weight must be reduced to a minimum by eliminating all equipment and supplies that are not essential.

b. The following factors affect the organization of a unit employed in jungle operations:

(1) Objectives of military importance are widely separated and consist primarily of airfields, seaports, and lines of communication.

(2) Large-scale overland operations are limited and units larger than division size are rarely employed.

(3) Due to terrain and restricted road nets, combat units will require less than normal organic transportation. Organization of carrying parties composed of our own troops, or utilizing friendly nationals, must be considered. Supply lines may be short in terms of distance, but long in terms of time.

(4) Terrain, vegetation, and weather conditions limit the use of heavy weapons and equipment, requiring in some instances the addition of special type equipment.

7. Command

While unity of command must be continually maintained, the difficulties of terrain, visibility, and weather so complicate control that its decentralization is an acknowledged characteiistic of jungle operations. Jungle combat is primarily one of many separate engagements conducted by small decentralized units. Leaders of small units must be thor-

oughly trained in leadership and self-reliance and all men must be thoroughly briefed in the mission of their unit.

8. Logistics

Logistics in jungle operations are characterized by rapid deterioration of all classes of supplies, difficulty in movement, the importance of keeping supply points close behind advancing troops, the increased emphasis that must be placed upon preventive medicine, and the extreme need for the practice of supply economy by all personnel. Proper security of logistic installations must be a continuing operation, since jungle warfare is conducive to infiltrations, guerilla action, or raids.

CHAPTER 2 OPERATIONS

Section I. GENERAL

9. General

a. The principles of combat in the jungle do not differ from those of combat in other areas. The techniques of applying these principles, however, are modified to suit the terrain and the conditions of the area.

h. Forms of maneuver for operations in the jungle approximate those employed in normal open terrain operations. Penetrations, envelopments, and infiltration are performed as in open terrain. (For detailed information, see FM's 7-10, 7-20, and 7-40.)

c. Because of the difficulty of maintaining control, it is essential that the mission and the plan of attack be understood by all personnel. Detailed briefing is a "must."

10. Standard Operating Procedure

a. Because jungle operations are decentralized in nature, it is necessary that effective standing operating procedures be established to insure the attainment of maximum control. Standing operating procedures for jungle operations should provide instructions to be followed in the absence of instructions to the con-' trary, but should include only those details which lend themselves to standardization without loss of effectiveness. The various means and effectiveness of communications are limited and must be reserved for essential traffic. To off-set this limitation, both administrative and tactical considerations must be included in unit standing operating procedures to expedite and facilitate operations and minimize confusion.

b. The scope of standing operating procedures for jungle operations resembles that for other type operations. For a further discussion of standing operating procedures, see FM 101-5.

Section II. EFFECT OF JUNGLE ON OPERATIONS

11. Observation

Limited observation in a jungle makes contact and control most difficult. This difficulty must be offset by assigning narrower frontages, reducing distances . and intervals between individuals and units, increasing patrol activity, and permitting greater freedom of action on the part of the small unit leader.

12. Communication

Climate and terrain peculiar to the jungle do not change the basic principles governing communication systems, but they do affect the various means. Wire. communication assumes a more important role due to limitations placed on the other means of communication. The effectiveness of radio is reduced by dense vegetation and climatic conditions. The lack of suitable trails limits the use of motor messengers. Visual signals normally employed to lift artillery fires and emergency prearranged signals cannot be depended on because of limited visibility. Prearranged sound signals provide an excellent means of communication for security detachments and patrols. The use of organic means of communication is fully discussed in Chapter 4.

13. Transportation

In most tropical areas, vehicles can be used in coastal regions and on inland plantations where roads have been constructed. During the rainy season, native roads may become impassable. Tracked vehicles are better suited for jungle operations; however, they, too, are limited to the coastal regions until roads have been cleared through the jungle. (See par. 89.)

Section III. FACTORS INFLUENCING JUNGLE TACTICS

14. Movement

Movement in the jungle is calculated in terms of time rather than miles. When movement is by foot and the terrain is difficult, progress is slow. It is not uncommon to spend 2 hours of hard travel in traversing a distance of one-half mile through the jungle where roads, trails, or tracks are not available.

15. Support

The difficulty of movement and the weight of equipment, weapons, and supplies decrease the speed of the supporting arms and services. This forces the foot troops to reduce their speed accordingly. Tanks may be used against definitely located targets, where the terrain permits. Small tank units may be attached to infantry units for the reduction of enemy strong points.

16. Flank Security

Flank security in the jungle must be continuous. Because of difficulties of terrain and vegetation, flank security units cannot easily maintain a uniform rate of march, and proper dispersion is often times limited. The noise of movement through undergrowth and of cutting trails may warn the enemy of their approach. The speed of a column is greatly reduced by the frequent' change of security elements that have to move to the front and flanks and rejoin the column as it passes.

17. Supply

The supply of ammunition, food, and equipment that can be maintained regulates the advance of the combat forces. Where the primary means of supply is hand carry by troops, the length of the carry should be kept to a minimum. Natives may be used in some areas over greater distances, carrying larger loads for longer, periods. Usually, such use of natives will require extremely good supervision, organization and control to obtain efficient operations. The rapid deterioration of all classes of supply adds to the problem of resupply.

Section IV. TROOP MOVEMENTS AND MARCHES

18. Rate of March

a. The rate of march depends on the type of jungle traversed. In dense jungle it is not measured in miles per hour, but in hours or days. Where vegetation permits, the column speed may be about 1% miles per hour where no trail breaking is needed. When there is no trail, the rate of march depends on the speed with which one can be cut.

b. Commanders must be constantly on the alert to keep the rate of march and the length and number of rest periods in line with the physical endurance of the unit. Physical exhaustion reduces mental alertness, which makes a unit susceptible to surprise and defeat.

c. Extreme temperatures make frequent halts almost mandatory. Generally, at least 15 minutes rest out of every hour is required. Precipitous trails, dense foliage, and other terrain obstacles may compel a 10-minute rest every half-hour. The heat and humidity are factors which will affect every march to an unpredictable extent. (See FM 21-11 for detailed discussion on adverse effects of heat.) Men should be allowed to drink when thirsty to avoid dehydration. Water requirements may amount to as much as two gallons 2?er man per day. March j^lans should therefore provide for water resupply during the march.

d. Animals accompanying a column of foot troops can, in most instances, maintain the same rate of march. However, they should not be kept under pack more than 8 hours a day, and their cinches should be loosened during the noon halt. Poorly trained pack animals traveling on narrow jungle trails require constant checking. They catch their loads on trees and vines, and their lashings and cinches must be adjusted at every halt, and frequently between halts. Requirements for forage must be csnsidered in operational planning.

e. Resupply may be performed by .transport helicopters, allowing the troops to travel lighter than would otherwise be possible. Helicopter scouting parties can speed the march by on-the-spot selection

of routes. (See chapter V for detailed discussion of supply problems.)

19. March Discipline

a. March discipline is made difficult by the problems of control. Dense forests and vegetation will present a serious barrier to effective control, not only on a march but in any type of movement. To get trooj)S to the proper j)lace at the proper time in condition to successfully accomplish the mission, requires the utmost ingenuity and leadership of the commander.

b. Difficulties of control through lack of direct observation of the major portion of the march unit must be offset by reduced distances and intervals between individuals and units, increased jDatrol activity, and added responsibility of the small unit leaders. Definite march objectives must be assigned and each unit leader must be acquainted with the complete march plan. As an expedient, telephone wire may be laid by the lead element of a march column so that elements throughout the column can use it as a means of communication.

c. When a column uses a single trail for any length of time it tends to become impassably muddy, even in the "dry" seasons. Additional trails must therefore be cut and the impassable area avoided. The noise of cutting can seldom be detected more than 40 yards away in the jungle. Forward patrols and chopping details must be rotated frequently.

d. Another solution to the march problem is to have separate columns moving at the same time and speed on parallel routes toward the march objective. This formation keeps the unit more compact and

304492°— 54 2

Figure 3. This jungle growth is so thick that men must maintain close contact or get lost.

better deployed for action than a single, strung-out column. and helps to prevent the trails from becoming mud bogs.

e. March discipline demands good leadership and control among the small unit leaders. To minimize the control problem, all men should observe the following rules of conduct:

(1) Prescribed distances must be maintained on a jungle trail (fig. 3). The distance between men and between elements of a column will be less than under normal conditions. Jungle trails are often narrow and confined by walls of brush on both sides or by precipitous cliffs rising sharply on one side and often dropping off a hundred feet or more on the other. To prevent loss of contact, all members must be alert to prevent the accordion action that occurs so often on a march. Loss of contact can mean loss of life and ultimate loss of a particular campaign. Additional connecting files are often required to maintain contact.

(2) Men leave the trail and stand motionless on the approach of aircraft.

(3) At halts, men relax, physically; they can never afford to relax mentally. Security guards are posted facing outward, If trails intercept the route, patrols must be stationed on them until the entire column has passed.

/. The column commander should be stationed near the front of the column so he can deal quickly with any situation. He should always have with him some means of communicating with all elements of the column.

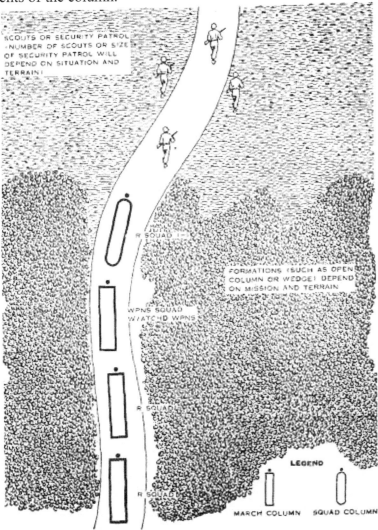

Figure Jf Column formation for jungle operation.

g. To control the direction of march, one person per column or trail is designated to use a compass. Each platoon leader is responsible for the direction control of his platoon and each leading platoon provides for its own security to the front (fig. 4).

20. Selection of Routes

The selection of usable routes is a difficult job. A straight line is rarely the most practicable way between two points in a jungle. (See par. 71.)

  a. Old maps can seldom be depended on for accurate trail routes since trails change due to erosion, fallen trees, swollen streams, and landslides. Every patrol should be instructed to note and report all variations from existing maps.

  b. Aerial photographs will seldom show trails in the dense growth, but a good photo interpreter can pick out salient features of terrain which will aid in terrain evaluation and orientation. The natives will normally have small gardens of sugarcane or breadfruit or palm trees that can be detected in photos. Small, characteristic white dots or dashes between villages are trails.

  c. It is safe to assume that trails exist between villages, even though none appear on available maps. Natives will often blaze a trail, and troops should learn to recognize these signs. "Where does this trail go?" will elicit a more accurate answer than "Does this trail go to so and so?" A native usually gives an affirmative answer to any "yes" or "no" question. When enemy contact is not imminent and speed of movement is important, existing trails and stream beds should be used. The danger of ambush along existing trails is always greater than at any other place in the jungle. However, good patrolling and the use of loyal native guides and trained dogs will reduce this danger.

  d. Streams may be used as trails if not too deep or swift, and one of the fastest and most dependable means of jungle travel is by small boats on available waterways. Since unforcable streams must frequently be crossed, men and pack animals must be trained in water crossing. Loads should be removed from pack animals and towed across.

21. Selection of March Objectives

  a. March objectives vary with any mission in any particular situation. Where ambush is an ever-present factor, each halt may be considered a march objective and the location of a position for the halt should be selected with great care. When a march requires two or more days, the intermediate march objectives must be chosen with particular forethought. They should be recognizable on the map as well as on the ground and they must lend themselves to all-ai'ound (perimeter) defense.

  b. In planning march objectives, the intervening terrain barriers must be assessed at their full value as time and strength consuming factors. Night halts should be made with sufficient daylight remaining to establish and adequately secure the bivouac before darkness.

22. Night Marches

There will be times when the situation will necessitate a night march. Night movement of any kind is very difficult, especially from the standpoint of control, and requires detailed planning. When the stars are visible they serve as guides in keeping direction. However, when the jungle roof is so thick that the stars cannot be seen, night marches will generally follow well denned trails, and movements on or off the trails will be aided by the following expedients:

  a. Have the lead party string phone wire and each man follow the wire, holding it in his hand.

  h. Have troops close up and hold onto the pack or belt or a rope tied to the pack of the man immediately preceding. This prevents straggling and infiltration of the column by the enemy.

  c. White engineer tape may be laid by the lead party.

23. March Security

  a. Security measures used in jungle operations do not differ substantially from the measures taken in open terrain except that the distance between security elements is less and, because of reduced observation, more security elements may be needed to provide all-around protection for the entire march column.

i. Units must be security conscious during a march and at every break and halt. During all breaks and halts, the units move off the trail and face outward, and security elements are immediately sent out to protect the front, flanks, and rear of the column. If the halt occurs at a convergence or crossing of trails, patrols are sent down the untraversed trails for a hundred yards or more. These patrols remain in place until the column forms again and clears the crossing. Then the patrols rejoin the column, attaching themselves to the rear of the last march unit. The remainder of the march column should be given a rest. During the rest period all men keep their weapons nearby, prepared at all times to meet an enemy attack from any direction. The need for alertness cannot be overemphasized. If possible,

halts should be ordered only when a large portion of the column is on terrain that lends itself to defense.

24. Jungle Navigation

This paragraph concerns only the peculiarities of navigational problems in jungles. For determining direction without a compass, map reading in the field, and use of the compass, see FM 21-75 and FM 21-25.

a. Vegetation is the one major obstacle to jungle navigation whether by night or by day. Available maps can seldom be depended on for accuracy of trails, roads, villages, or even rivers. Through erosion, flash floods which carry everything before them, and quick growing vegetation, trails, and roads are erased from existence in a very short time. All the shortcomings of map and aerial photos can be overcome by training the individual soldier in jungle navigation and other aspects of jungle warfare.

~b. Navigation through jungles without roads and trails requires the utmost in map-reading ability and direction-finding skills: skill in following a predetermined route through terrain without obvious landmarks, and skill in being able to orient one's own location at all times in respect to the starting point.

o. The following procedures will help a unit to navigate a jungle successfully:

(1) Obtain a map (scaled to 1/25,000 or larger) that is up-to-date with the latest data from other units, patrol reports, and information obtained from natives; and have a good

. compass.

(2) Select the following minimum navigation personnel for each column: a map reader, a compass man, a man to record detail, and a man to measure distance. The duties of the map reader and compass man are self' explanatory. The detail recorder keeps a running account of unusual ground formations to help correct the map, and landmarks to aid future navigation. He records the compass reader's azimuth findings and the distance determined by the distance measurer and maintains a count of his strides. This recorded data enables the column to approximate its position at any time in relation to distance and direction from the starting point (fig. 5). (3) Move short distances at a time, 100 to 300 yards, frequently checking the map with the ground and patrol reports; and measure back azimuths with the compass when practicable. Direction once lost in the jungle is hard to regain. d. When lost in a jungle, the first and paramount action is to sit down and think out the situation calmly. There are numerous aids to navigation and many means of survival. This principle of sitting down first and attempting to regain a bearing before crashing off through the jungle has saved many patrols as well as aircraft pilots who were forced down in jungles during World War II. Knowing and acting on the following suggestions may save the life of anyone who is lost in a jungle:

(1) Follow streams towards their mouths.
(2) Select a distant, distinct terrain feature for orientation as you move. This will keep you from walking in a circle.

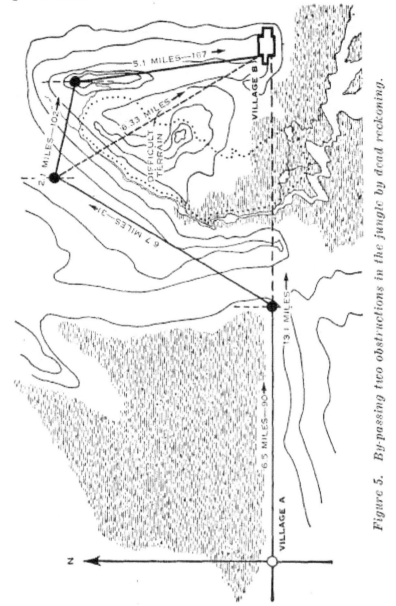

Figure 5. By-passing two obstructions in the jungle by dead reckoning.

(3) Recheck every compass setting and computation for errors, and correct them. e. Assigned aircraft should be used in every possible way to help ground units to navigate jungle terrain. The utility helicopter is suited to this type of operation. In sparse jungle it can act as a reference point or traffic direction vehicle while hovering or circling, and it can act as a radio relay point. For extensive operations, special homing devices may be issued for use by troops and aircraft.

25. Bivouacs

a. Because of the nature of jungle terrain bivouac areas are usually of battalion or smaller unit size. Bivouac areas are prepared for all-around defense, with suitable fields of fire. Patrols are sent out for a distance of 800 to 1,000 yards on all trails leading to the bivouac area, to determine if any enemy troops are nearby. Security elements are stationed on all roads, trails, and stream beds leading to or near the bivouac area. Frequently, the length of the column will compel it to bivouac along the trail in depth. Figures 6, 7, and 8 show a suggested plan for movement into a bivouac area and the disposition of units within the area.

b. A bivouac site should be on high ground and convenient to a source of fresh water; and it should provide all-around protection. High ground is desirable for a bivouac, not only because it is more easily defended but because it is freer from flies, mosquitoes, and other insects. Also, it is better drained and cooler. A native village should seldom be selected as a bivouac site. The enemy may have the village under observation, or some of the villagers

```
        n
     FRONT
     -L+ •
     \ XX I
      XX/
      A —.
       \ V
      ( -WA
SIGNAL GIVEN HERE \
     —N M-f /
      * I ft I
SIGNAL GIVEN HERE XX
      XX
      XX
      NT
SIGNAL GIVEN HERE
      I I
     LL_t.
      —h
```

XX SCTS IN OBSN
1ST RIFLE UNIT (SQUAD-PLAT-CO OR BN)
2D RIFLE UNIT
3D RIFLE UNIT

Figure G. Movement from column into bivouac (any sine unit),

may be unfriendly. In addition, the unsanitary conditions of most native villages will expose troops to many diseases.

c. Listening posts are established in foxholes along the outer edge of the perimeter defense. Two- or

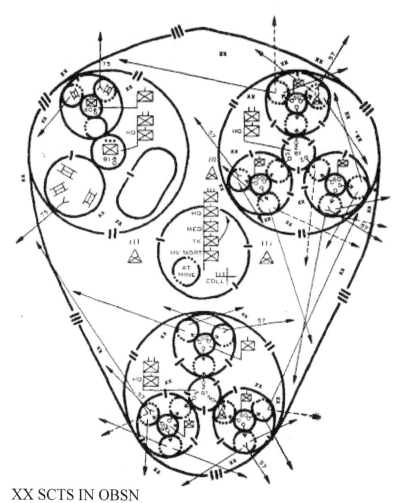

XX SCTS IN OBSN

Figure !'. Perimeter disposition (schematic) of weapons and units within the regimental combat bivouac.

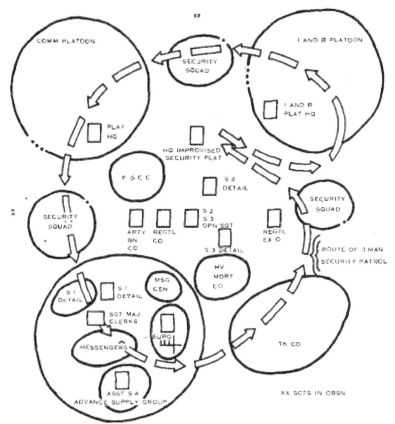

Figure 8. Perimeter disposition (schematic) of elements of the regimental command post.

three-man foxholes are preferable to a one-man foxhole because they allow the occupants to take turns at observing and listening, and permit comradeship which has a high morale value. Necessary patrolling is carried on between the listening posts. Men should be trained to identify the normal night sounds of the jungle. Warning devices in the form of antipersonnel mines and trip flares may be installed around the perimeter of the bivouac.

Section V. OFFENSIVE COMBAT

26. Influence of Terrain

a. Operations in the jungle preclude the degree of centralized control which may be maintained in open terrain. Combat becomes a series of decentralized small unit engagements. Subordinate unit commanders must exercise initiative and be allowed freedom of action in executing a mission.

b. Because of the lack of adequate routes of communication, the few existing roads and trails are the focal points of most jungle combat. Commanders always try to seize such features and deny their use to the enemy.

27. Movement to Contact

Most moves in the jungle are executed to contact or to maintain contact with the enemy, but there are certain basic considerations incident to a movement to contact that do not apply to a normal march:

a. Supporting weapons, particularly automatic weapons, must be well forward so that as soon as contact is made the force of supporting fire may be brought quickly to bear.

b. Lead elements must be especially alert to pick out and fix the enemy positions in time for the commander to quickly estimate the situation and decide how best to employ his unit.

g. Strict march discipline is necessary in any movement to contact to avoid disclosing the presence of the troops prematurely.

28. Approach March

a. The march is often restricted to single file, even for large units, unless trails are cut. Flank protection for moving columns is often impossible, and security forces work at greatly reduced distances. The rate of march will be governed by the condition of the trail and, in general, time factors will be increased and space factors decreased.

h. When the position of the enemy has been determined and contact is imminent, the final stage of the approach march is made on a wide front, even though this takes a great amount of time. The formations used in open warfare are suitable, but the distances and intervals are decreased in proportion to the degree of visibility. Advance guards normally precede the formation at a distance of 50 to 100 yards. The advance is by bounds, from one terrain feature to another. Skirmish lines are not used by leading elements until contact is made. The commander must always be prepared to employ his mortars and other supporting weapons, since meeting engagements are common in the jungle. Discontinuous resistance must be disposed of rapidly by leading elements.

29. Reconnaissance

a. In a jungle operation, reconnaissance is limited in scope but must be continuous and progressive in nature. A commander depends more on patrol reports in making plans for jungle operations than in any other type combat. A thorough reconnaissance is made ahead of and to the flanks of an advancing column, and ground reconnaissance always precedes an attack. It will not always be possible
to determine the state of development of an enemy, but the extent of the enemy's defensive area can usually be ascertained.

b. Although aerial reconnaissance is restricted and ground reconnaissance slow, a combination of the information gathered by these means is of great assistance to a commander.

30. Orders

The attack order should emphasize the objective and routes to the objective in detail because observation is so restricted. Because of the inherent decentralization of control, all leaders must be thoroughly informed of the plan of attack, and must be given a wide latitude in executing their part of the mission.

31. Attack

a. Based on the information obtained from reconnaissance, the commander decides on the point and direction of attack; preferably against the enemy's flank or rear. If time is limited, it may be necessary to start an envelopment without complete reconnaissance. It may take hours or days for the enveloping force to reach its attack position. A small enveloping force in the enemy's rear and astride his supply trail will probably cause him to withdraw.

b. The enveloping force moves to its attack position in one or more columns. Patrols are sent forward to confirm the hostile positions. The attack is conducted as in open terrain with the formation similar to that used in a night attack. Distance and intervals are reduced and the column formations are maintained as far forward as possible.

c. Fire support is as essential in the jungle as in open terrain. Unsupported infantry cannot breach a defensive position without incurring heavy casualties. The area to be breached must be pinpointed. Artillery and mortar forward observers may have to approach within extremely short range of their own fires. If there is the likelihood of confusing the registering rounds of units the fire support coordination center (FSCC) will control the priority of units to register with smoke shells or by sound sensing. Artillery fires are often adjusted by sound sensing. Adjustments are often made by creeping. When the artillery fire terminates or shifts, the mortars may continue firing to cover the movement of the infantry from its assault position.

32. Assault

a. During the preparatory fires, the assault infantry may have to withdraw a short distance. Artillery forward observers and a few men of the attacking unit will remain forward under cover. During the assault, supporting fires should continue until they are masked by friendly troops. They are then shifted to cover specific targets which will most assist the progress of the assaulting force. The assault force advances by assault fire. The enemy must be kept off balance and given no opportunity to recover or to reoccupy positions.

b. The success of an attack is determined by the manner in which the assault is executed. Hesitation invariably results in avoidable casualties. Too early development, however, results in premature loss of control. Under ideal conditions, it is possible for

troops to crawl within a few yards of their supporting fires without danger. These fires are then shifted beyond the objective or to cover the flanks of the assaulting force. On penetrating the position, the assaulting force moves rapidly toward its objective, employing assault fire to overcome scattered resistance and prevent the formation of a local counterattack. As the interior of the position is likely to be cleared and more open, the formation should spread out. Eeserves may be used to widen the gap. When the objective has been taken, reserves complete mopping up; the mop-up must be thorough. If the attack is ordered to continue, a small holding detachment should be left on the objective so the enemy cannot reoccupy it.

33. Coordinated Attack Against Prepared Defense

a. When attacking a system of defended localities, it may be expected that heavy bunkers, protective and tactical wire, and antitank and antipersonnel mines will be encountered.

b. The enemy must be burned or blasted out of his bunkers and pill boxes. This requires a great amount of fire power. In attacks against positions of this type, the frontages must be narrow to insure the greatest possible concentration of fires. As in all jungle attacks, limited objectives must be established or control will be lost.

c. The preparatory phases of such attacks involve the construction and improvement of roads and trails behind friendly lines, the movement of supplies and ammunition, and the coordination of all arms and weapons that are to be used to support the attack.

d. If naval gunfire can be used to advantage, it should be requested, and a schedule of the fires worked out in advance. A naval gunfire liaison team may assist in directing the gunfire by direct ship-to-shore communication.

e. Arrangements should be made for maximum artillery preparation and continuing artillery support. The artillery may require several days for displacement to new and better positions, and registration.

/. Forward air controllers make ground reconnaissance, employing all possible means to locate accurately the targets for preparatory bombing and strafing attacks.

. g. Continuous air-photo reconnaissance provides stereopairs for daily study. Terrain or sand table models of the area to be attacked are excellent aids in briefing leaders.

h. Every attempt should be made to capture prisoners for questioning before the attack. The close jungle terrain favors an ambush and small patrols can sometimes ambush enemy parties on trails. Such patrols usually consist of not more than three or four men, all of whom must be experienced jungle fighters and expert riflemen. A steady flow of prisoners at all times is highly desirable for intelligence purposes.

i. Patrolling must be continuous and an aggressive attitude must be maintained. Constant patrolling secures information, keeps the enemy on the defensive, inflicts casualties on him, and limits his patrolling.

j. Before the attack, artillery, mortars, and naval gunfire attack known and suspected enemy targets. Fires may be lifted at a prearranged time or on a

prearranged signal. When the fires of the heavier guns are shifted to deeper targets, the mortars and artillery in close support of the infantry continue their fires. As the fires of the indirect supporting weapons are lifted or shifted, the direct fire weapons of the assaulting units increase their rate of fire and move onto the objective using assault fire. Mopping-up units follow the assault waves closely. Such units search out stragglers and blow up emplacements. During the period of reorganization and preparation for further advance by assault units, mopping-up units hold the ground gained.

k. The capture of the objective must immediately be announced by prearranged signal so that previously planned protective fires may be brought down on call.

34. Meeting Engagement

a. In a meeting engagement, the commander who first estimates the situation, arrives at a decision, issues his orders, and executes his plan, enhances his chance of success. By rapidity of action, he seizes the initiative and gains surprise.

h. The nature of the engagement and the limited observation may require the commander to base his estimate and decision on very limited information. To await additional information might result in loss of initiative. But when there is opportunity for a reconnaissance, even though limited, it must be made. Patrols investigate the extent of the enemy's position and try to determine his strength.

c. If emplaced artillery is supporting the column, it should be used as soon as possible if the enemy appears to be in strength.

d. 60-mm mortars bring short-range fire to bear as quickly as possible. Control is by voice or sound-powered telephone.

e. As soon as 81-mm mortars are emplaced, they are assigned tai-gets. Their fire is controlled by the fire direction center and adjusted by forward observers who use radio or telephones.

/. If the commander decides on an envelopment, the enveloping force moves out rapidly. Orders are always oi'al. The commander indicates his desires as briefly as possible, illustrating on maps, air photographs, hasty sketches, or diagrams traced on the ground.

g. The enveloping force must always indicate by prearranged signal when it is in position and ready to assault. If wirelaying teams can keep up w T ith the enveloping force, the signal will be transmitted by wire. Signals can be transmitted in the clear once the enveloping force is detected. If no wire can be laid, the signal may consist of prearranged colored flares or any other available visual means. Flare signals should be repeated. Signaling by flares or by firing weapons may disclose the position of the enveloping force, and the psychological factor of total surprise, which frequently can be achieved in the jungle, is lost.

h. The following features common to meeting engagements should be noted:

(1) There is no stage of development of the column. The troops move from route column to assault positions.

(2) Artillery and mortar fire is brought down on the enemy immediately upon contact and he is held under as great a volume of ac-

curate fire as possible during movement of the enveloping force.

(3) The enveloping force must move rapidly but, at the same time, must arrive at the assault position in physical condition to enter the fire fight.

(4) If aircraft are to be used, the leader of the enveloping force must know it, and the

pilots must be carefully instructed as to the areas, times, and direction in which they are to make bombing and strafing runs.

(5) If supporting fires are being delivered, the commander of the enveloping force must give the signal for lifting them.

(6) Reserve elements protect the rear and defend against enemy counterenvelopments. If not required for such purposes, the reserve elements may be used to exploit a success or extend an envelopment, but they should always be held out initially until the situation is developed.

35. Coordinated Attack Against Hastily Organized Position

Attacks against a r ;.stily organized position are -similar to the operation described in paragraph 34. Single or double envelopments are used when possible. The following points should be noted:

a. Reconnaissance can often determine the location of automatic weapons. The lateral extent and depth of the enemy position may also be ascertained by .small ground patrols.

b. Since time is available to locate and fix the

enemy position, supporting aircraft may be employed on close support missions.

c. The attack must be conducted from objective to objective so that subordinate leaders and commanders may regain control frequently and reorganize. For a platoon, the distance between objectives may be reduced to as little as 100 yards; visibility is the governing factor.

36. Night Attacks

Night attacks in dense jungle present difficulties of control; however, the possible surprise effect of a night attack frequently makes such an operation worthwhile. The techniques of executing night attacks are set forth in FM 100-5, FM 7-10, FM 7-20, and FM 7-40, but these techniques will have to be modified frequently for jungle fighting.

a. The number of columns into which the assaulting units are divided ordinarily depends on the number of existing trails within the zone of action leading toward the eiiemy position. To cut new trails beforehand is a slow, noisy process likely to warn the enemy of the impending attack. While small groups of experienced men may move quietly through the jungle, large groups are likely to be detected. It is possible for one or more small assault parties to move through the jungle, but night movement is ordinarily confined to trails, stream beds, or similar features easily identified and followed.

~b. Coordinating the time of attack is difficult and allowance must be made for delays, even when the column moves on trails. Landmarks and easily distinguished features will be scarce or entirely absent. Because of the dense overhead growth, pyrotechnic

signals may not be seen by all column leaders, and dampness and heat may make the pyrotechnics un-dependable. A preliminary reconnaissance and a careful analysis of the conditions under which the attack is to be made will help the commander perfect coordination.

c. Night attacks are small-scale and have limited objectives. Where suitable avenues of approach exist and mobile troops are available, a movement around the hostile position at night, followed by early morning attacks against hostile rear areas and installations, may prove a major factor in the defeat of the enemy.

d. Preliminary reconnaissance, the use of guides, the identification of distinguishing marks, and the control of noise is more difficult than in daylight. The assault force will be in no danger of observation, for troops will not cross open skylines, fields, or highways. Detailed briefing of all commanders, down to squad leaders where possible, should include map reconnaissance, and terrain reconnaissance during both day and night. Night terrain reconnaissance is extremely important, so that squad leaders can select objectives under the same conditions that will be present during the planned attack.

e. Reserves are placed in a position to best assist the assaulting echelon. They may be located along the trails so that they can quickly strike a hostile force in the event of a counterattack.

37. Offensive Ambushes

a. Ambushes are an effective means of waging offensive combat in the jungle. Vigorous employment of carefully executed- ambushes is an economical means of inflicting heavy casualties on the enemy and reducing his effectiveness by decreasing his mobility. A force which is trailbound, which tends to close up while moving, which maintains inadequate security, or whose noise gives warning of its approach is particularly susceptible to ambush. The effectiveness of ambush relies upon the surprise delivery of close-range fires. Closely coordinated fires should come from at least two directions and should converge on the target. Primary and alternate routes for rapid withdrawal of the ambushing party must be previously selected and reconnoitered because the ambush will invariably attract other nearby enemy troops. Assembly points for the ambushing party must be designated so that on signal to withdraw, the men can do so rapidly and without confusion.

b. To achieve surprise, fires of the ambush party should begin only on a prearranged signal. Furthermore, all firing should cease and withdrawal should begin promptly on a predetermined signal. After entering the ambush areas, the route followed by the ambushing party while going into position should be carefully inspected for evidence of the party's presence ; the evidence should be removed. If possible, the ambush area should be entered from the rear. When-time and circumstances permit, antipersonnel mines should be emplaced beside the ambush area so that when the enemy seeks cover from the ambush fires, he will contact the mines. A ruse is sometimes needed to cause the enemy to close up in the area of converging ambush fires. A piece of equipment or some unusual disturbance of the vegetation or terrain in the desired spot will frequently arouse his curiosity, and, unless he is very cautious, cause him to move to the decoy and enter the sector of fire selected by the ambush party. To achieve an added degree of surprise, it is desirable to select an ambush position which is not necessarily tactically sound. The sacrifice of observation and fields of fire will be more than compensated for by this increased surprise. It is good strategy to occupy the ambush position before daylight.

c. Because of the frequent employment of ambushes in jungle operations, all units should be trained in their techniques. Such training should include the selection of positions, occupation and organization of the position, conduct of the ambush, and planned withdrawal.

d. Where time allows, careful rehearsals, carried out under command supervision, should be held.

38. Patrolling

a. For the general principles of patrolling and the detailed instructions concerning the operations of patrols, see FM 21-75.

b. The size of a patrol varies with each mission assigned and should include only the number of men necessary to successfully complete the mission. A patrol may consist of only two or three men, or it may be a company or even a battalion. The larger patrols are used primarily to establish patrol bases from which smaller patrols are sent. The force at the patrol base provides men to bolster the strength of the smaller patrols when they become involved in a fire fight they cannot handle. This system saves considerable time since patrols do not have to be sent out each time from the position of the main forces. This is especially important in jungle terrain where distances are measured by the time it takes to traverse them and not by the miles covered.

c. A basic principle of jungle patrolling is to guide on roads or trails, but to avoid their use. The enemy will usually place automatic weapons fire on these routes and establish listening posts near them. Jungle patrols ordinarily use the column formation and the single file because paths are so restricted. Dense jungle growth often prevents the dispersion to the flanks needed for the diamond formation. Because security is in depth with little or none to the flanks, it is necessary to send security elements as far forward as practicable to avoid being ambushed. At halts, flank security is obtained by sending elements to the limit of visibility in all directions.

d. A patrol can sometimes choose a long, circuitous route to an objective that will let it move faster and easier than a more direct route that goes over denser terrain and swamps. Guiding on prominent terrain features is not always possible, so the compass must be relied on to an unusual degree. At least two people on a patrol should have a compass and be well qualified in its use. Maps, even though inaccurate, may still be indispensable. All personnel must be proficient in reading maps and aerial photos.

e. The equipment needed by a patrol varies with each mission, but it should be kept light. One machete is often enough of all that can be used at one time for cutting a path. Weapons are handled with special care.

Section VI. DEFENSIVE COMBAT

39. Influence of Terrain and Vegetation

a. Defensive combat in jungle terrain does not differ in principle from defensive combat in other types of terrain. For principles governing defensive combat, see FM 100-5, FM 7-10, FM 7-20, and FM 7-40.

b. The extent to which a defensive position is developed requires an understanding of jungle characteristics. There are no impenetrable jungles, impassable swamps, unfordable rivers, or unscalable cliffs. The commander who assumes that his command is protected by such barriers invites disaster. Because of the heavy vegetation and dense undergrowth, observation and fields of fire are restricted. Commanders at all levels must make a thorough terrain analysis of any area they are to defend.

c. The actual development of the defensive position depends on the time available for construction purposes, and the material, equipment, and troops available.

d. Thorough and continuous ground reconnaissance is necessary because of the limited effectiveness of security elements and the concealment from air observation afforded the enemy. Dense jungle imposes severe limitations on the defensive use of weapons because observation is often limited to a few yards. These factors, along with the restrictions on maneuver and control, place the greatest emphasis on planning, coordination, and small unit leadership.

40. Organization of the Ground

a. The principle of all-around defense of the position is strictly observed. The limited fields of observation allow the enemy to approach the position without being detected. Infiltration is easier and there is greater danger of attack from any direction.

b. Battalions and smaller units often operate as independent units. When operating alone, units are prepared to defend against any enemy attack from any direction. The extent of all-around defense depends on the type of operations, the units involved, and the terrain.

c. When possible, one or both flanks should rest on a natural obstacle such as a river, lagoon, swamp, steep cliff, or the sea. While such features constitute obstacles to the attacker, they are never considered as insurmountable barriers and provisions must be made to meet with fire the enemy who attacks over them.

d. Mutually supporting defensive positions are established whenever possible. Limited fields of fire and limited observation may make it difficult to establish such a position. If this is the case, then a "shoulder to shoulder" perimeter defense is desirable because it closes the formation to such an extent that enemy infiltration is difficult.

e. The first step in organizing the ground is to place the automatic weapons and clear the fields of fire. Alternate and primary positions are constructed. Overhead cover should be provided as soon as possible, particularly for automatic weapons.

/. Camouflage is continuous and strict camouflage discipline is observed. Vegetation is not cut un-

necessarily and the cutting is carefully planned and controlled by leaders. Instead of clearing open fields of fire for automatic weapons, fire "tunnels" should be cut. The standard fire lanes disclose the automatic weapon positions, but fire tunnels make their positions hard to locate.

41. Security

a. Security is planned to gain early information of the enemy's approach. Patrols, sentinels, observation posts, listening posts, and outposts are used. Outposts must be strong enough to delay the enemy and prevent him from attacking before the main battle position can be alerted. Sentinels within the position give early warning of infiltration by the enemy.

h. Trip wires connected to rattles, antipersonnel mines, or illuminating flares may be installed around the position at night to warn of the enemy's approach. Other means may be used to illuminate the battlefield at night; cans filled with jellied gasoline with a remote control system of ignition may be placed in strategic areas and ignited when the enemy approaches. Such illuminations should be located far enough from the position so that the light will not blind the defenders nor illuminate them for the enemy. Illuminating shells may be fired by mortars, artillery, and naval guns. Searchlights, also, may be used to illuminate the battlefield.

c. Companies responsible for the defense of the outer areas of the perimeter send out combat and reconnaissance patrols. Routes to be used by patrols are changed frequently.. Patrolling is continued during hours of darkness. Detailed planning and

coordination must be effected by all commanders sending out night patrols. Plans include the mission, time of departure, time of return, routes to be used, sign and countersign, and emergency signals. Patrol plans are sent to the next higher headquarters and to the direct support artillery headquarters for coordination with adjacent units and securitjr elements forward of the main battle positions, and with supporting artillery fires.

42. Conduct of Defense

The defense of a perimeter is conducted as in any other type terrain; see FM 7-10, FM 7-20, and FM 7-40.

a. Long-range fires are planned and executed as in any other type of terrain, conforming to the desires of the commander and the availability of ammunition.

h. Close defensive fires are planned and fires to destroy the integrity of an enemy's force before he launches his assault; and the artillery, mortars, and crew-served weapons within range of enemy forces can support the troops on the main line of resistance.

c. Company commanders have the authority to call for final protective fires covering company areas. Control of fires of infantry organic weapons is decentralized to the extent required by the frontages of the battle position, the terrain, and the limits of the higher commander's observation. Units whose defense areas are not under attack or whose weapons are not required to fire in support of areas which are under attack, discipline their fire to prevent disclosure of their positions.. The decreased frontages, shorter distances, and closer intervals between units

in jungle operations call for extensive and detailed planning for this phase of fire.

43. Counterattack

Plans are made and movements are rehearsed for counterattacks to restore positions which might be penetrated by the enemy. Intense mortar and artillery concentrations in preparation for such counterattacks are planned. Counterattacks are launched before the enemy has had time to consolidate a position he has succeeded in taking.

44. Defense Against Ambush

a. The best defense against enemy ambush is skillful patrolling in advance of a unit. Native scouts and trained dogs are invaluable for this purpose. Observance of strict trail discipline is essential for defense against ambushes. Men should not—

(1) Close up along the trail.
(2) Straggle.
(3) Talk in a loud tone.
(4) Lose contact.
(5) Kelax vigilance.

b. Although a unit may be surprised by an ambush, rapid movement for only a short distance will usually place it beyond immediate danger. The ambushing party should be enveloped rapidly. Speed will disorganize the ambushing party but delay may result in casualties for the ambushed units. A plan should be prearranged for the immediate deployment of a unit in case of ambush from any direction, and every member of the unit should be thoroughly familiar with this plan and his part in it. The plan must be thoroughly rehearsed under combat conditions.

Section VII. RETROGRADE MOVEMENTS

45. General

If the mission and situation do not require a defense in place, a retrograde movement, particularly in the presence of an aggressive and stronger enemy, may be the most suitable type of action. Denying the enemy the use of roads, trails, and other avenues of approach, and disrupting his lines of communication as he seeks to advance, may so harass, discourage, and exhaust his troops as to decrease materially their effectiveness and permit a decisive counterblow by friendly forces. Smoke is useful for screening retrograde movements, especially in open areas. All supplies and equipment that must be abandoned are systematically destroyed to prevent their use by the enemy.

46. Withdrawal

a. Cover and concealment provided by the jungle facilitate withdrawal by units in contact with the enemy. Small groups familiar with the routes over which they are to move can deny these trails to the enemy and force him to attack on a narrow front or make him cut trails around the delaying groups. This delays the enemy long enough to allow the main body to withdraw. Withdrawal by daylight in jungle areas has many of the advantages of a night withdrawal in more open terrain, and it permits a greater degree of control. However, personnel and equipment moving on wide trails easily observed from the air offer favorable targets to hostile combat aviation.

b. In dense jungle areas, delaying action is executed principally on and near trails. In open areas, this action frequently, requires the occupation and defense of one or more delaying positions. The flanks of such delaying positions must be protected against envelopment by the enemy.

c. Small, well-trained groups can delay forces many times their size; however, since this type of combat is especially strenuous, units should be divided into groups which may alternate in occupying delaying positions and thus obtain rest, while the enemy is kept constantly engaged. Forward observers remain with the delaying force to adjust fires.

d. In addition to their normal equipment, delaying groups should carry axes, mines, and explosives. In order to cause the maximum delay, particularly of vehicles, bridges should be destroyed and trees and other obstacles placed across all trails and roads as far forward from the delaying position as time and the situation permit. Mines should be placed in the jungle on both sides of obstacles, and in the obstacles themselves, to make the removal of the obstacles hazardous. Booby traps are especially suitable for this purpose. At all points where the jungle is thin and does not offer an obstacle to the movement of foot troops, mines may be employed. Mines emplaced at random along trails and paths will cause the enemy to move with caution and will delay his progress. Obstacles should be placed along the front of the delaying position in such a manner that the enemy movement will be canalized into areas where the delaying force can place the most firepower.

e. Because of the difficulties of supply and coordination, small forces are better suited for executing delaying action in the jungle. Reserves should be available behind leading elements along each trail to support these elements, and to patrol the trails to. prevent them from being cut off.

CHAPTER 3 EMPLOYMENT OF SUPPORTING ARMS

Section I. INFANTRY

47. General

a. To obtain the full value of concentrated firepower from supporting weapons, commanders must determine how and to what extent they can overcome the limitations imposed by the jungle on the mobility, visibility, and control of the infantry's organic supporting weapons. Not only is it hard to solve these problems; in addition, good firing positions for direct fire and indirect fire weapons are comparatively hard to find in dense jungle and in grass areas.

b. In jungle fighting, it is not advisable to assume that every sound or movement to the front is made by the enemy, either in attack or defense; it might be a small friendly unit that has strayed from its assigned zone into the adjacent unit's line of fire. All units must include in their standing operating procedure the circumstances under which individual and crew-served weapons fire on targets that are not definitely identified. The SOP should establish methods of maintaining lateral contact and must prescribe specific procedures for obtaining the current location of adjacent units.

c. The employment of infantry weapons in night defense must be standard within each unit. The.

enemy will invite fire on small probing units in an effort to locate weapon positions. Therefore, the commander must insure fire discipline at night within the perimeter and prescribe the conditions under which each type weapon will open fire. These conditions must be understood and adhered to by weapon crews and the leaders of supported units.

48. Tank Company

a. Although tank operations in jungles are comparatively restricted, tank support may be decisive.

b. The normal attachment of one or more tank platoons to each battalion with subsequent attachment of one or more platoons to a rifle company is valid in jungle operations. However, limited visibility often makes it desirable to break down the tank platoons into sections for attachment to rifle platoons. When open areas provide the opportunity, the tank platoon should revert to the usual role of attachment to a rifle company.

o. The methods of coordinating infantry-tank team attack described in FM 7-35 are applicable in the variety of terrain defined as jungle, except that infantry protection must operate more closely with tanks in a dense jungle (fig. 9). Tanks fire only on specific targets requested by the infantry, and prior planning on methods of fire control and target designation must be complete. Radio is the most efficient means of control and coordination for infantry-tank teams, but individual infantrymen also use the external tank telephone to maintain direct contact with the tank commander.

    d. When targets cannot be unmistakably designated by voice, the infantry points them out to the

Figure 9. The infantry must operate closely with tanks in a dense jungle.

tanks by tracer bullets or pyrotechnics. Tanks use their machine guns for reconnaissance by fire.

    e. In dense jungle, when little or no enemy armor is being encountered, tanks should be held in rear of the infantry to be brought up when heavy resistance is met. Engineers should be immediately available to help clear routes for tanks.

/. Coordinated reconnaissance has an even greater importance than on conventional terrain. The tank leader accompanied by the engineer leader recon-neiters all possible routes. When in contact with the enemy, a tank leader goes with leading elements to select the routes and possible targets for tanks moving behind the infantry.

g. The amount of engineer support required will be determined by the number of natural and man-made obstacles in the zone. Bulldozers or tank dozers may be required to clear routes, level stream banks, and tow tanks when necessary.

h. See paragraphs 64-66 for additional information on tank unit employment.

49. Mortars

a. Emphasis must be placed on the employment of mortars in jungle operations. Fire control and the transportation of weapons and ammunition are difficult, but careful planning will overcome these obstacles. When artillery cannot be emplaced, mortar fire combined with the direct fire of recoilless rifles must be used to the maximum extent consistent with the available ammunition supply.

b. The tactical employment of all infantry mortars is the same as on normal terrain. Although general support is the preferred method of employment, these weapons will more often be attached to the assault units, due to difficulties of observation and range limitations. Control of their fires can be maintained only by continuous emphasis on liaison, communication, and observation. An increased number of observers must be used and all unit leaders must have a working knowledge of observed fire procedures and the means of communicating fire requests.

c. Observers working directly in the front lines may have fires delivered with accuracy close to the leading troops. To do this with safety, the normal bracketing method may be replaced with a creeping adjustment, and the first round must be fired at a range that will give a positive over. Smoke rounds may help the observer to make the initial registration, but he frequently has to adjust by sound.

d. Special care must be taken to select firing positions with mask clearance. When fires are to be delivered in close proximity to friendly troops, shells must not detonate on foliage above them on the downward arc of the trajectory. When tree bursts make mortar fire ineffective against defensive installations, the delay fuze is used.

e. Mortars of all sizes are used to place fires immediately ahead of troops attacking in dense jungle. These fires must be closely controlled by reliable communication.

/. Preparatory fires from mortars have a casualty and harassing effect and will expose enemy installations by blasting away foliage and camouflage. Mortar fire against pillboxes or bunkers not only exposes the target, but destroys enemy troops occupying protective positions in the vicinity or causes them to move into other positions, making them good targets for direct fire or automatic weapons.

g. The survey party of the heavy mortar company must be trained to obtain data to supplement jungle maps. In dense jungle, front-line elements are often unable to relate their ground position to map positions or determine hostile positions shown on the map. Prearranged fires may be employed to orient a commander by having one mortar fire on a prearranged point that appears on the observer's and the front-line commander's maps.

50. Machine Guns

a. In all but the thickest jungle, the value of machine guns in supporting both offensive and defensive operations outweighs the difficulty in transportation and ammunition resupply. The successful employment of machine guns in providing continuous support for assault troops depends on taking maximum advantage of the time available for reconnaissance; the selection of suitable firing positions; the selection of routes of supply and displacement; and good control. Although these factors apply in any situation, their importance is underlined in jungle operations where each factor is complicated by the terrain.

 b. Jungle terrain does not materially alter the employment of the light machine guns of the rifle platoon's weapons squad; they should remain with the platoon.

 c. Firing positions and available fields of fire rarely permit the machine-gun platoon of the heavy weapons company to be employed in general support of the battalion. Because of the terrain, machine-

gun sections are advantageously attached to rifle companies or rifle platoons. As in other operations, commanders must decide which of the section's weapons will be taken forward from the off-carrier position. Experience has shown that the heavy machine gun can be successfully kept forward, but sometimes single guns will have to be used, as opposed to normal section employment. In this case, the guns which are left behind can be sent forward as trails are improved.

 d. Where enemy snipers or observers in trees are being encountered, it is advisable to place a heavy volume of machine-gun fire into the trees immediately in front of the advancing assault elements. When the leading elements mask this fire, it is shifted to the flanks.

 e. Machine guns also give valuable support to assault teams engaged in reducing enemy bunkers or cave positions. They combine their fires with those of the recoilless rifle in direct fire on the objective to permit the assault team's advance. These fires are shifted to the flanks (particularly to similar emplacements which .offer covering fire) when the assault teams approach the objective.

 51. Recoilless Rifles

 a. The accuracy, mobility, and striking power of recoilless rifles make them valuable as supporting weapons for jungle operations. They are especially useful in reducing cave positions, pillboxes, and bunkers frequently found in the jungle. In all operations, care must be taken to' select firing positions for recoilless rifles that provide safety from and prevent disclosure of the positions by the back-blast.

 h. The mobility, light weight, and low silhouette of the 57-mm recoilless rifle make it ideal for use with front-line infantry troops, both in static and mobile situations. It can be used to great advantage by maneuvering units of squad size or larger to destroy enemy machine-gun emplacements, pillboxes, and caves which might hold up their advance. In static situations, the rifle can be dug in on the front line to engage enemy installations of all types which may be holding up the company or battalion. The peculiarities of the jungle will require in the majority of cases that one 57-mm recoilless rifle be attached to each rifle platoon, with section employment in general support being exceptional. The weapon enables the platoon leader to effectively neutralize targets which otherwise would have to be reduced at close range with grenades, flame throwers, or demolition charges. In selecting positions for recoilless rifles, the location of friendly troops, safe routes of approach for ammunition bearers, and covered routes to alternate positions must be carefully considered. In dense jungle, the weapon position should be moved frequently. In broken or hilly jungle terrain, the recoilless rifle may be emplaced in a defilade position just in rear of the topographic crest of hills occupied by front-line troops. In this type of position the flash and debris caused by the back-blast are not so discernible to the enemy.

 c. The 75-mm recoilless rifle has great accuracy, mobility, and tremendous striking power. These characteristics make it an ideal weapon for reducing enemy installations; it may be more effective on these targets than indirect artillery fires.

d. The 75-mm recoilless rifle. is employed with front-line troops in the densest jungle and up to 500 yards to the rear in open and broken terrain. Firing positions are selected with due consideration for ammunition supply, which is a primary limitation on the use of the weapon in the jungle, and for the security of the piece.

e. In fast moving attacks, both of the 75-mm recoilless rifles of a section can rarely be used. The greatest effort should be directed toward keeping the ammunition supply on vehicles as far forward as possible.

/. Defensively, the 75-mm recoilless rifle is employed, insofar as possible, as in normal operations. When the weather and terrain prohibit the use of tanks in their antitank role, the 75-mm recoilless rifle my assume this mission.

g. The 105-mm recoilless rifle is preferably employed in general support and is assigned its primary mission of antitank defense.

Section II. ARTILLERY

52. General

The principles of artillery employment in jungle operations conform closely to the tactical and technical principles covered by FM 6-20 and FM 6-101.

53. Limitations

The use of artillery is limited by typical jungle characteristics: poor ground observation, lack of roads and open areas for gun positions, logistical difficulties, and climatic conditions.

54. Coordination With the Infantry

See FM 6-20.

55. Positions

a. Battery positions usually have to be carved out of the jungle and are small and compact. Logs from cleared areas should be saved to construct gun emplacements and personnel shelters. The swampy condition of the terrain may often make it impossible to dig adequate gun emplacements and slit trenches.

b. Since the jungle affords excellent concealment for raiding parties, all artillery positions must provide ample security against enemy infiltration. Good security demands a perimeter defense around each installation, an effective warning system, coordination with adjacent perimeter defenses, and frequent patrolling beyond the perimeter.

g. In coastal areas, suitable positions may often be found on the beaches, around plantations, or on nearby islands.

56. Observation

a. Forward observer teams are seriously handicapped by restricted visibility, and suitable observation posts are hard to find.

(1) Forward observers must remain constantly with the supported unit even if it means leaving high ground when the supported unit advances.

(2) Forward observers should, where the jungle terrain permits, cooperate with the aerial observer for the utmost effectiveness in verifying the location of troops and in obtain-

ing positive sensing of initial rounds and completion of the fire mission. (3) In making adjustments, forward observers should consider the height of the trees and the slope of fall of projectiles. i. Air observation is restricted over jungle terrain, but may be used to good advantage to—

(1) Observe for enemy activities such as movement over water or cleared areas on land.
(2) Give the general location of enemy installations.
(3) Locate enemy artillery positions.
(4) Observe and adjust artillery fires.

57. Offense and Defense

See FM 6-20 for the principles of the employment of artillery in the offense and defense. (Displacements may be very difficult, due to lack of roads and suitable position areas.)

58. Targets

Targets are hard to find. After locating suspected targets, although requiring the expenditure of large quantities of ammunition, it may be necessary first to blast away jungle undergrowth by means of air bursts and tree bursts before maximum effect on the target can be obtained.

59. Ammunition

a. Special care must be taken to protect ammunition from dampness and deterioration in tropical jungle climate.

5. The selection of types of ammunition and fuzes for jungle targets is the same as for similar targets in normal locations except that—

(1) Time fuze adjustment is difficult even in open areas because of the high grass.

(2) The burst from a proximity (VT) fuze is difficult to sense in adjustment when the trees form an overhead canopy. The performance of this fuze is apt to be erratic due to the excessive moisture in the air and on the ground.

(3) The delay fuze is valuable for obtaining bursts near ground level when foilage is high and thick.

(4) Smoke or WP is valuable for use in adjustment.

(5) Base ejection smoke may be used for close air support marking.

60. Communications

a. Wire is the most reliable means of communication for controlling artillery in jungle, operations. However, it is difficult to install and maintain. Light wire can be laid on top of foliage by liaison planes or helicopter.

b. The range of radios is shortened by jungle growth, but this problem may be resolved by using radio relay stations.

61. Fire Control

Fire control is centralized whenever possible; however, decentralization of control will be necessary as the density of the jungle increases.

Section III. ANTIAIRCRAFT ARTILLERY AND NAVAL GUNFIRE

62. Employment of Antiaircraft Artillery

a. General. The basic tactics and techniques involved in the employment of antiaircraft artillery will not change greatly in jungle operations. See FM 44-2, FM 44-4, and FM 101-5. Extensive detailed planning is required in advance of an operation to determine the amount, type, and most effective employment of antiaircraft artillery. Air defense must be provided for ports, beachheads, and advanced bases which are the starting points for offensive jungle operations. As the operation progresses air defense must be planned and provided for installations, troop concentrations, and other activities in open areas subject to aerial observation and attack. AAA defenses fall into two general categories:

(1) Installations subject to ground attack. In the early phases of an operation AAA deployment is limited by a defendable perimeter. AAA must remain within the main perimeter or be provided with a strong local defense. AAA should be emplaced to fire on surface targets as well as aerial targets.

(2) Installations relatively secure from ground attack. These conditions are encountered in defending existing installations in friendly territory or the expansion of defenses in captured territory well behind the combat zone. The preparation and occupation of such defensive

positions is relatively deliberate. Position areas should be selected to maximize the capabilities and min-imize the limitations of equipment employed. Eoads may not be present and sites may require extensive preparation at the time position areas are selected. Roads and sites should be completed before occupation. Local security must be provided but is not a primary factor in this type defense.

b. *Medium and Heavy AAA.* Normally there will be a requirement for medium and heavy AAA at ports, beachheads, and other areas used as the forward base for jungle operations. Since medium and heavy AAA is dependent on radar for fire control, their siting is much more critical than light AAA. The size and weight of equipment present serious problems in movement through jungle. Until such, time as medium and heavy AAA defenses can be installed, tactical aircraft must be depended on to defend forward installations from high level aerial attack. Medium and heavy AAA sites should be selected to optimize fire control system coverage for air defense. In the defense of shore installations weapons can frequently be sited to fire on waterborne targets in addition to their air defense role. Construction equipment must be available, not only to prepare roads and sites prior to occupation, but to maintain, improve, and expand the defense. Requirements for construction equipment and personnel are much greater in jungle than other type operations.

c. *Light AAA.* Light AAA is more mobile and has fewer technical limitations than medium or heavy AAA. It will therefore be employed more extensively than medium and heavy AAA in the early phases of an operation. There will be fewer areas requiring light AAA protection. Concentrations of materiel and personnel are greatly restricted in jungle areas. Jungle areas provide better means of passive defense. The overall requirement for light AAA will depend on the individual operation. Although the number of defended areas will normally decrease in jungle operations, those subject to attack will become increasingly vital and may justify a higher level of defense than similar installations in another type operation.

d. The most critical aspects of employment of AAA are the need for reconnaissance in considerable detail, the requirements for extensive clearing of fields of fire, and the inaccessibility of optimum positions. This may prevent the attainment of the optimum level of defense desired by limiting the number of weapons that may be employed in a defense area. Further, terrain considerations may require decentralization of control.

63. Employment of Naval Gunfire

The principles of employment of naval gunfire are the same as for normal operations, with the exception that observation will be limited. At times, observation may be possible only from the air.

Section IV. TANK UNIT EMPLOYMENT

64. Mission

The mission of tank units in the jungle is the destruction of the enemy by using firepower, maneuver, and shock action.

65. Tactical Employment

a. Jungle operations prescribe small tank units, close coordination with other arms, and extensive and detailed planning. Generally, the tank company or platoon is the largest tank unit employed in the jungle, but, occasionally, tank units of battalion size may be feasible.

1). Just as the extremes of terrain found in the jungle affect the size of the tank unit employed, so does it proportionately increase the amount of coordination necessary between combat arms. Each tank needs dismounted infantry to give it close-in protection from tank hunter teams and dismounted enemy. Engineers are essential for road construction, for stream and river bridging, and for many other engineer tasks which tanks may require to retain mobility. When tanks are separated from the dismounted infantry, fixed and variable time artillery fires over the tanks in the assault give them close-in protection. In all phases of jungle combat, the tank is an integral part of the combined arms team of infantry, engineers, and artillery.

o. Planning is a part of all operations; however, in the jungle, many phases of planning take on added importance. Rehearsals should be conducted over terrain similar to that of the objective area. Plans for reorganization after an attack should include the selection and designation of rallying points for tanks. These rallying points should be located in the vicinity of the line of departure and be readily accessible to tanks for resupply and refueling.

d. For a more detailed discussion of the tactics and techniques used by tank units in jungle operations, see FM 17-32 and FM 17-33.

66. Effect of Extreme Heat

Tanks are designed to operate efficiently at temperatures up to 160° Fahrenheit. The tank crew, however, is adversely affected by the heat and humidity. Excessive heat combined with fumes from the tank motor and armament reduces crew efficiency. The crew is easily fatigued, and more than the usual amount of time must be allowed for tank maintenance and resupply. Crew members are rotated in jobs within a tank to insure a balanced work load for all and to improve their efficiency.

Section V. ENGINEERS

67. Road Construction

a. The speed with which jungle operations are conducted is affected more by engineer effort than in normal operations. In temperate zones, the progress of the infantry usually depends upon how fast their units can overcome enemy resistence, and the ability of the engineers to keep up with the most rapid advance. In nearly all jungle areas, roads are relatively undeveloped: they are usually narrow and winding and incapable of supporting sustained military traffic. Therefore, the bulk of engineer effort centers around the construction and maintenance of roads and trails.

b. There are numerous factors that complicate road construction in the jungle. The heavy rainfall in these areas imposes a drainage problem of major concern. Wherever possible, low ground should be avoided in laying out a road. When it is impossible to by-pass low swampy ground, it will be necessary

to construct long sections of corduroy road. It is advisable to cut the right of way much wider than normal so the sun can dry out the road bed. The enlarged right of way also provides room for the construction of the ditches necessary to keep the subgrade drained.

c. The engineers need heavy construction equipment. The bulldozers authorized for the division engineer battalion are often inadequate, and additional bulldozers and other construction equipment must be procured from supporting engineer units or installations. If the road net will permit, an alternate route plan is set up so that main roads or sections of them may be closed when they need major repairs.

68. River Crossings

a. The cover afforded by the jungle enables troops to be brought up with secrecy for a river crossing, but road conditions usually limit the movement of heavy bridging equipment. Fords are unclependable since rain can make them impassable in a short time.

b. Another factor which makes bridging difficult is the rapid rate of decay of wooden bridges. This makes it necessary to incorporate a large safety factor in the initial construction of such a bridge. Initially, prefabricated bridging including panel type and the decks of floating bridges may be used to bridge short gaps.

c. The floods that can be expected during rainy seasons may wash out a bridge several times during an operation. A tremendous quantity of debris accompanies flooding on a jungle river, and the debris damages bridge bents. Therefore, bridges should be designed with the minimum number of spans necessary to carry the estimated loads. In the coastal plains, the streams frequently shift their courses, leaving bridges on dry ground with the stream flowing elsewhere. Attempts at dredging a channel to confine the stream are often unsuccessful since the stream quickly fills the channel with silt and overflows in another direction.

69. Water Supply

Water sources are usually abundant, but untreated water should not be drunk because of pollution. A special problem exists in areas where the water is contaminated by the blood fluke. The fluke enters the body through the pores of the skin and engineer personnel working in the contaminated streams are particularly vulnerable to attack. See FM 21-10 for methods of purifying this water for drinking purposes. When the fluke is known to be present, bathing and wading in ground water must be avoided.

70. Mine Warfare

Since the jungle itself is an effective obstacle against vehicles, antitank mines and other anti-vehicles obstacles are normally confined to roads, trails, and occasional patches of cleared ground. Antipersonnel mines are usually incorporated into defensive plans to delay and divert the enemy and to serve as warning devices.

71. Mapping

Because of the inaccessibility of jungle areas, adequate maps are scarce, and those that are available are frequently inaccurate except for the location of coast lines and principal rivers. The numerous unnamed swamps, streams, inlets, and lagoons are seldom indicated, and contours, if shown, are seldom accurate. The trail nets shown can seldom be depended on because trails are rapidly grown over and new routes take their places. Native towns and villages frequently bear native names entirely different from those on the maps. This is also true of many terrain features. Any information that can be used to correct existing maps should be forwarded to the appi-opriate headquarters for prompt dissemination. Engineer reconnaissance to supplement the data on maps is of prime importance. The engineers should obtain information on the following topics:

a. Location and condition of roads and trails.
b. Location of road construction and building materials.
c. High water level of streams.
d. Condition of banks at river crossing sites.
e. Location of water sources for drinking, laundering, and bathing.

72. Planning

In planning for a jungle operation, the unusual demand for heavy construction equipment must be considered. The engineers determine what additional equipment is available from special lists and how it may be procured. The jungle provides an abundant supply of timber and it is often desirable to establish a sawmill to provide lumber. Provisions should also be made for treating the piling and other bridge material to retard decay and withstand the ravages of termites. Sand bags disintegrate rapidly in the jungle, and when they are used, a supply must be available for replacements.

Section VI. CLOSE AIR SUPPORT

73. Doctrine

The doctrine for the employment of air forces in open areas is equally applicable in the jungle: see FM 31-35 for Air-Ground Operations.

74. Target Identification

Close air support targets located between the bomb line and friendly positions must be accurately identified to the striking aircraft before the attack. Either a target director post or an air control team furnishes the target identification and controls the air strikes. A forward air controller may identify a target for aircraft through any one or a combination of the means indicated in a through h below:

a. Reference to grids or coordinates on large scale maps or mosaics.

6. Reference to nearby landmarks or terrain features readily discernible by the aircraft pilot.

g. Artillery smoke shells, including base ejection smoke shells.

d. Artillery illuminating shells to designate target areas at night.

e. Radio homing and beacon equipment.

/. Adjustment of simulated air attacks to definitely orient a pilot.

g. Use of any one or a combination of the foregoing methods to orient a tactical air coordinator who, in turn, leads attacking aircraft to the target. The tactical air coordinator should have a means of marking the target.

h, Colored smoke rifle grenades or white phosphorous mortar shells.

75. Control

a. When the forward air controller cannot observe well enough to control air strikes, the tactical air coordinator may assume this job. The tactical air coordinator can increase the effectiveness of close support operations by locating targets before the combat aircraft arrive in the objective area. When suitable multiplace reconnaissance aircraft are available, it is desirable to have the ground commander or his representative accompany the air coordinator to advise on ground force preferences.

b. Location of friendly front lines is of vital importance in close air support operations. This can and must be accomplished through use of panels, colored smoke, or identifiable terrain features apparent to the pilot.

Section VII. CHEMICAL, BIOLOGICAL, AND RADIOLOGICAL WARFARE (CBR)

76. General

The doctrine and principles for employing CBE agents, and the methods of protection from enemy use of these agents in jungle terrain are the same as in other terrain. Detailed discussions of offensive and defensive CBE warfare are to be found in FM 3-5 and FM 21-40. The techniques of employment and defense that are peculiar to jungle warfare are discussed in paragraphs 77-81.

77. Chemical Agents

a. Persistent chemical agents such as mustard gas (HD) are extremely effective in a jungle when used against unprotected troops. High temperatures and low winds help to create very high vapor concentrations of such agents. Extensive foliage tends to break up liquid concentrations, although drops and splashes of liquid agent on foliage near the ground present a long term hazard to personnel in the area.

b. Nonpersistent chemical agents are effective in the jungle, except that phosgene (CG) is rapidly absorbed by the lush vegetation. Cyanogen chloride (CK), although less toxic than CG, is not absorbed by vegetation and has been known to persist in casualty producing concentrations for as long as 4 hours in jungle forests. In the jungle, a given weight of CK covers three times as much area as the same weight of phosgene. The G-agents have excellent characteristics for use in the jungle since they tend to be relatively persistent, are about twenty times as toxic as phosgene, and are not effected by the high humidity or absorbed by jungle vegetation.

o. Chemical agents can be used effectively in mining and booby-trapping jungle trails used by the enemy or those leading into our own defensive positions; in bombing or shelling assembly areas, bivouac areas, and enemy installations; and in preparing defensive fires. When chemical agents are used in the defense or in preparation fires, the protection available to friendly troops must be considered since even nonpersistent agents will linger in the target area and its vicinity. Chemical agents can be used in the jungle to neutralize or destroy islands or pockets of enemy resistance which may then be by-passed, and nonpersistent agents are particularly effective against enemy bunkers, cave positions, and similar strong points.

d. Artillery shells and aerial bombs with delay fuzes are probably the best means of delivering chemical agents in the jungle. Artillery and mortar tree bursts over forty feet in the air result in the complete loss of the agent; the average loss of agent when delay fuzes are not used will be about 25 percent. Aerial spray is only about ten percent effective. Chemical land mines, when used, should be protected from rust; fuzes and detonators must be protected from moisture and mildew. Care must be taken that trip wires are not fouled by rapid growth of jungle foliage. Munitions requirements for persistent and nonpersistent chemical agents in the jungle are found inFM3-5andFM3-6.

78. Smoke and Flame Weapons

a. Smoke may be used for signaling, for marking targets, and for providing smoke screens, curtains, and blinding smoke on enemy installations. Colored smoke grenades, shells, and smoke streamer rifle grenades are useful for signaling or marking purposes. Limitations on visibility in the jungle will govern their use. For example, smoke streamer rifle grenades projected above the jungle canopy may not be visible to ground troops, but they can be useful as signals to air observers and to specially located ground observers.

b. Smoke screens and curtains produced by mechanical generators, smoke pots, shells, or aerial bombs may be used to limit air and ground observation when the vegetation and tree top canopy are not dense enough to give concealment. Smoke sprayed from airplane smoke tanks will generally be ineffective in jungle operations because of turbulent air currents above the jungle canopy which rapidly disperse the smoke. Smoke curtains produced by artillery and mortar shells can be employed effectively by ground troops in the attack. Individual bunkers and isolated strong points can be blinded by the use of HC and White Phosphorous (WP) grenades prior to the assault. HC and WP may have an incendiary effect, so fire hazards should be considered before using them. White phosphorous also has a casualty effect which may be desirable. Munitions requirements for ground and air smoke munitions are found in FM 3-5 and FM 3-6.

o. Flame weapons are used effectively in the jungle to cause casualties and to destroy the natural concealment and camouflage afforded by the vegetation. Flame throwers, artillery, mortars, rockets, and fire bombs delivered by tactical air are all effective methods of employing flame weapons, including incendiaries, in this type of terrain. Flame land mines, prepared locally from empty fuel drums or other containers filled with thickened fuel, can be used defensively against infiltrating or attacking enemy forces to provide warning, for casualty effect, and for battlefield illumination.

79. Biological Agents

Biological agents can be used effectively in the jungle. These agents include living organisms, the toxic products derived from some of these organisms, and certain chemicals which have a detrimental effect on plant life. Among the latter are regulators which affect the growth of the plant and defolients which kill the plant by causing the leaves to drop off. Chemical plant agents can be used to destroy the enemy's food crops and the natural camouflage of the jungle and to mark bomb lines for tactical air and other boundaries. Defolients have been used successfully to expose to air observation trails which are likely to be used by guerrillas or enemy patrols. For a detailed discussion of biological warfare and possible agents, see TM 3-215.

80. Radiological Agents

Radiological warfare is as effective in a jungle as elsewhere. Vegetation can retain contaminating radiological agents for long periods, and decontamination is extremely difficult.

81. Defense Against CBR Attack

a. The means and methods of protection against CBR attack outlined in FM 21-40 and FM 21-45 are effective in the jungle.

o. The protective mask and permeable protective clothing are tolerable in jungle terrain and climate. Limitations on vision imposed by the mask combined Avith personal discomfort as a result of wearing the protective equipment may decrease individual efficiency and even present a morale problem. Prior individual and unit training in CBR protective measures carried out in jungle terrain is particularly important in order to overcome or allow for these problems. Such training can be most effectively given without scheduling extra time by integrating it into the individual and unit training schedule. See paragraphs 108 and 119.

g. Special precautions must be observed to maintain unit defensive equipment in a usable condition against the threat of mildew, rot, and rust.

CHAPTER 4 COMMUNICATION

82. General

a. All of the organic means of signal communication are employed in the jungle. The lack of good trails often restricts or even prohibits the use of vehicles. Therefore, light signal equipment should be substituted for heavy bulky equipment when possible.

b. Wire should not be laid prematurely and should be recovered when possible. Batteries deteriorate rapidly in the jungle even when not in use: approximately twice the normal battery requirement may be anticipated.

c. While all equipment for use in the tropics must be capable of functioning efficiently in a high temperature, temperatures alone do not cause the greatest difficulties. Wetting by salt water or salt spray in landing operations and inadequate storage facilities cause much damage. Continuous damp, warm air causes a general disintegration of types of insulating material.

d. Fungus growth often reduces insulation resistance to such an extent that service is interrupted. Under tropical conditions, fungus may form in a day or two on the edges of insulators, and in keys and jacks, causing short circuits. Insects also create maintenance problems. Spiders may build webs in switchboard wiring; even lizards have been known to enter equipment and short circuit main bus bars. Termites destroy wooden structures and some types of insulation. Tropical wind storms sometimes carry large quantities of dust which get into equipment and cause contact and insulation trouble.

e. Before beginning jungle operations, every possible measure must be taken to dry out and protect equipment. The care of signal equipment is of special importance in the rainy season. It should be moisture-proofed and fungus-proofed to provide protection against fungus growth, insects, corrosion, and salt spray. The treatment, which is designed for field application, consists of spraying or brushing on a moisture- and fungus-resistant varnish. Even after this treatment, additional precautions should be taken. Waterproof covers are an added protection. If covers are not issued, they can be made from salvaged material. Signal equipment should never be placed on the ground and left there for long periods.

/. When pack animals carry signal equipment, frequent inspections are made to see that the equipment is traveling securely. When time permits at halts, the equipment and lashings should be examined and tested.

83. Wire

a. The limitations imposed by the jungle on the other means of communication cause a greater de-23endence upon wire. Wire routes are limited and the few available routes will be heavily traveled, making overhead construction imperative in most cases. The talking range of wire on long lines may

be reduced due to moisture. Expedients to overcome this may include the use of telephone repeaters or use of a twisted pair for each side of the circuit. Increased capability of enemy infiltration makes telephone security particularly important.

b. In a fast moving situation, it may be difficult to maintain wire communication, but wire teams should follow attacking elements as closely as possible.

c. Wire communications in attack and defense will generally follow the procedure set forth in FM 7-24.

84. Radio

Although radio communication in the jungle is highly desirable, particularly in the attack, its normal operating range is seriously reduced by dense vegetation and adverse atmospheric conditions. Radio operators must be trained to copy weak signals and to use every expedient possible in siting and constructing antennas. Remote control of equipment may be helpful in gaining a more favorable location of the radio set. Radio sets may have to be man-transported and hand-operated. Substitution of man-packed sets for vehicular sets may be necessary.

85. Messenger

a. The messenger is one of the most reliable means of communication in jungle operations, particularly in lower units. Except when roads are available, motor messengers will be of little value. Messengers should be carefully selected men with a high degree of intelligence, courage, and aggressiveness. Their training should include instructions in jungle lore, trail knowledge, map reading, evasion and escape,

and the use of the compass. Trails blazed with code markings materially assist messenger communication. In dense and difficult jungle, foot and motor messengers are employed in pairs. In the battalion, company, and platoon, messenger communication is one of the primary means. In the defense, it supplements wire communication. A number of men should be trained to replace messenger casualties.

b. The use of aircraft for messenger service is dependent on suitable landing facilities. The helicopter is most desirable for this purpose, since it requires little space for landing and taking off. Aerial drop and pickup techniques may be used with fixed-wing aircraft where the terrain does not afford a suitable landing field.

c. Trained homing pigeons are a reliable agency of messenger communication in the jungle; however, darkness, rain, and other adverse weather conditions decrease their efficiency. Their rate of flight is about 40 miles per hour.

d. Trained dogs are used satisfactorily in jungle operations both as scouts and messengers.

86. Sound Communication

Sound can be used to great advantage in the jungle, particularly as a prearranged signal for security units and patrols. For additional information on sound communication, refer to FM 7-24.

87. Visual Communication

a. Visual communication includes the transmission of messages by flags, panels, and pyrotechnics, but its use is limited by the density of the jungle. Areas in which panels may be used are scarce.

b. Semaphore and wigwag flags can be suitably employed in jungle operations. Flags may be obtained from available stocks, or may be improvised. Flag stations must be located to deny observation by the enemy, and they should have a contrasting background against which the flag will stand out clearly.

c. While it is fundamental that lamp signals are sent only from front to rear, situations will occur in jungle operations in which such communication is permissible in both directions. Lamp stations should be concealed from enemy observation, and will generally be located along straight stretches of trail. Either white or red beams may be used. In general, the white beam is visible at greater distances by night; the red beam by day. In fog and smoke, the red beam is more satisfactory. A flashlight with an improvised reflector may serve as a signal lamp, or a lantern with an improvised movable cover may be used: the cover is lifted to expose the light for long or short periods to represent dashes and dots.

d. Visual communication by pyrotechnics is not satisfactory in areas of heavy vegetation; it is seldom possible to project them through overhead foliage. If pyrotechnic signals are to be used, lookouts should be detailed to watch for them.

CHAPTER 5 SERVICE AND SUPPLY

Section I. GENERAL

88. Importance and Special Conditions

a. The importance of maintaining supply and the special conditions affecting it in jungle warfare limit the extent of operations, rates of movement, and the strength of the forces employed. The availability of trails, roads, and waterways; the density of natural growth; the season; and general terrain conditions have a direct influence on the types of transportation that can be used and, consequently, on the functioning of supply. Supply requirements must be anticipated well in advance of actual needs. Careful planning is necessary to conserve transportation facilities, and the control of all classes of supply must be closely supervised in order to exclude surplus and nonessential items.

b. Unit supply officers must be experts in advance planning and in forecasting needs: replenishments must be requisitioned well in advance; reconnaissance of supply routes and watering points must be continuous; and alternate routes and supply points must be located and developed.

c. The jungle affords concealment from air observation and, since it is easier to protect convoys from ambush in the daytime, commanders should move supplies during daylight hours.

d. Special provision must be made to protect supplies from spoilage caused by climatic conditions. Tentage, tarpaulins, or thatched shelters are necessary to provide protection from heavy rains and hot, tropical sunshine.

89. Transportation

a. The basic means of jungle transport is hand-carry, though pack animals are frequently employed. Jungle vegetation is not satisfactory forage for domesticated animals, so a large part of their load must necessarily be food for them. Native pack animals and handlers may be used to supplement organic means and to preserve the combat efficiency of troops, but the dependability and maintenance of the natives must be carefully considered.

6. Air transportation is an important factor in the supply of jungle operations. Emergency supplies can be air-lifted to units when all other transportation fails. Army aircraft and helicopters have been employed with success in supplying isolated patrols and small units. When the supply planes cannot land, they may deliver supplies either by parachute or free drop. Amphibian planes may be used when suitable water areas are available.

c. Waterborne transportation is the most economical and often the surest means of supply. Streams, lagoons, and other waterways should be used to the maximum extent possible. Supplies transported over waterways are less susceptible to loss or damage, fragile containers are safer, and the destruction caused by insects is largely avoided. Boats, canoes, and rafts are the most practicable types of water craft to use. Distributing points should be established along waterways to save transportation by men, animals, and vehicles.

d. Wheeled transportation is generally impracticable except on roads (and in the dry seasons on wide trails) and in areas where the jungle growth is light. Engineer and pioneer troops can improve trails to permit movement of ^-ton trucks and trailers in areas close to the combat echelon. Track laying vehicles are generally reliable in jungle operations and furnish one of the principal means of logistic support, however, they increase maintenance problems.

90. Classes of Supply

a. Jungle rations consist normally of nonperish-able canned and dehydrated items. The number of rations carried by the individual soldier will be determined by such factors as how and in what quantities food can be brought forward, when resupply will be effected, and the estimated duration of the operation. Hot meals should be served whenever possible, and individual or group cooking is encouraged when carrying parties cannot distribute hot food. Feeding is usually done during daylight because of the danger and difficulty of movement at night and the possibility of enemy night attacks.

b. Kapid deterioration is a primary consideration in class II supply items. Clothing, particularly shoes and socks, lasts a very short time. For items of this nature, requirements should be estimated well in advance and special provisions should be made for adequate resupply. Companies and similar units should carry a limited emergency supply of assorted sizes of shoes and socks. The troops and the limited transport capable of moving with the troops can carry only a few weapons and small amounts of ammunition. The amounts and types of weapons and ammunition to be carried are command decisions which must be made after careful consideration of the difficulties of transport and the types of weapons needed to accomplish the mission.

c. The supply of class III items does not initially present a great problem, as relatively few vehicles will be in operation. However, battalion and regiment will establish class III supply points for any vehicle that may be operating. The replenishment system is based on the exchange of empty 5-gallon drums for full ones as in normal operations.

d. The supply of class IV items will, for the most part, concern special items of individual and unit equipment. In many cases, the equipment normally authorized a unit will be augmented by additional allowances, and special items of clothing and equipment that are needed but not authorized may be obtained. The use of large amounts of special defense equipment in defensive positions is the exception rather than the rule due to difficulties in bringing up such materials.

e. Because of the weight and bulkiness involved, the supply of ammunition and explosives often presents the greatest supply problem in the jungle. The best solution is close control exercised by all leaders over ammunition expenditures within their units and the employment of the appropriate weapon for the fire mission. Company battalion, and regimental ammunition supply points are located close behind the front-line units to facilitate supply.

Section II. MEDICAL SERVICE

91. Employment

a. The manner in which medical units support their tactical organizations depends on the employment of the supported unit. Wide variations may be expected at division level and below, but above division, medical support is normal. The greatest variances will be found in the support of the infantry regiment by the regimental medical company, and with the support of the infantry division by its medical battalion.

b. The regimental medical company requires considerable augmentation when undertaking jungle operations. This is due to the extreme moist heat, location of tactical units supported, difficulty of traversing terrain with casualty loads, and a requirement to increase medical personnel attached to the tactical companies supported. This augmentation may best be accomplished by the commander requesting additional medical personnel, through channels, from field army units designed for this purpose. Plans to utilize native litter bearers, when available, are also established prior to entry into combat. Equipment may inquire modification to permit maximum efficiency in combat. This may include establishment of pack equipment for all medical installations, and the replacement of evacuation vehicles with tracked vehicles to negotiate the jungle terrain.

92. Battalion Medical Platoon

The company aid sections of the battalion medical platoon need increased personnel strength to permit more complete support of all companies of the battalion. (In normal operations no company aid men are attached to the battalion headquarters company or to the headquarters of any other company of the battalion.) Even more important is the augmentation of the litter bearer section of this platoon, because evacuation by litter is slow and exhausting work. Natives, properly supervised by trained medical service personnel, may be used as litter bearers. The battalion aid station is located in defilade, or with the best available cover and concealment, as close to the unit supported as the tactical situation permits. The aid station requires local security to protect its patients and medical personnel.

93. Regimental Collecting Platoon

The regimental collecting platoon transports casualties from battalion aid stations to the regimental collecting station where the casualties are treated. Usually, the collecting station can care for the regiment's casualties with the normal amount of personnel, and the ^-ton vehicles equipped with litter supports should be capable of handling their transportation. . However, at times, the litter bearers of the collecting platoon will have to evacuate the casualties of the battalion aid stations, and additional litter bearers will be needed to speed the evacuation to the collecting station. Natives are frequently available for this purpose.

94. Medical Company Headquarters

Perhaps the greatest problem of the medical company headquarters is that of resupply. The; medical system of property exchange must be closely supervised to prevent the stock of medical items from falling to a dangerously low level.

95. Division Medical Battalion

The division medical battalion may be called upon to support the regiments of the division on a division front or on regimental missions. The organization of the medical battalion makes it capable of supporting each regiment by attachment of a platoon of ambulances and one platoon of the clearing company to provide further medical care and treatment. The ambulances of the medical battalion may be replaced by other more maneuvei^able vehicles. Air evacuation from forward installations can be used to relieve surface transportation of part of its load and, at times, waterways afford a good route of evacuation. The medical helicopter ambulance unit provides an excellent means of evacuation in the jungle. Mobile army surgical hospitals perform immediate surgery" in the division area.

96. Evacuation

Higher headquarters evacuate the wounded from division installations using all available means. A continuing effort is made at all medical installations to return the fit to duty, and rapidly move the unfit out of the combat area.

97. Personal Hygiene

a. Good personal hygiene is more important in jungles than in open terrain, and it is harder to maintain. A determined and continuing effort by commanders at all levels must be made to provide sanitary facilities for their troops. The mere fact that troops are isolated in jungle areas for long periods of time does not justify letting the hair and beard grow, allowing clothing to become exceptionally dirty, and neglecting body cleanliness. Food handlers in particular must continue the high standards of hygiene which they normally maintain in garrison.

Military sanitation is imperative. Kitchen and human waste must be disposed of by acceptable methods, or diseases will quickly neutralize the fighting potential of an entire command.

98. Diseases in General

a. Troops arriving in jungle areas are exposed to many diseases with which they are not familiar. The level of sanitation in jungle areas and among the native inhabitants is frequently very low. Furthermore, there is often great difficulty in enforcing even the simplest sanitary regulations, as many natives are too ignorant, superstitious, and lazy to cooperate. Water supplies are grossly contaminated and there are no modern water supply systems. Rainwater catchments are used in some areas. Most natives use shallow, poorly protected wells, or drink from streams. There are no sewage systems, and natives are unwilling to use latrines. Animals and some natives-dispose of- body waste promiscuously, even directly into the streams used for drinking water.

b. The diseases of greatest military concern are malaria, filariasis (elephantiasis), intestinal diseases, venereal diseases, dengue (break-bone) fever, yellow fever, scrub typhus, and typhus fever. Of these, malaria is the most prevalent in all seasons. The common diarrhea and amoebic and bacillary dysentery are the most frequent intestinal diseases, but typhoid and paratyphoid fever also occur. Gonorrhea is the commonest form of venereal disease, but syphilis and granuloma inguinale are fairly prevalent. Fungus infections are frequent, as are other skin diseases. Tropical ulcers are particularly common. Parasitic infections, heat exhaustion, sunstroke, and pneumonia may affect small numbers of troops.

99. Insect- and Animal-Borne Diseases

Insect- and animal-borne diseases are those which are transmitted from man to man or from animal to man by a bloodsucking insect or animal. The germ may be introduced into the human blood stream or tissues during the bite of the infected insect or it may be deposited upon the skin by defecation or during the process of biting. In the latter two instances, scratching the insect bite infects the wound with the germs. The commonest insect and animal disease carriers are listed below, together with suggestions for combating them. Troops must follow the precautionary and preventive measures described in order to avoid infection.

a. Diseases Transmitted by Mosquitoes.

(1) Malaria, yellow fever, dengue (break bone) fever, filariasis (elephantiasis), and some

forms of sleeping sickness are mosquito-borne. Commanding officers are responsible for executing mosquito-control measures. Their decisions are based on the military situation and the recommendations of the medical service officers who make mosquito

surveys. For a detailed discussion of mosquitoes and mosquito control, see FM 21-10. (2) For individual protective measures, use mosquito nets, protective clothing, insect repellent, and insecticide aerosols. At semipermanent camps, large tents should be screened and sprayed with a residual insecticide. If malaria is present use suppressive drugs.

 b. Diseases Transmitted by Ticks.

 (1) Hard ticks transmit Eocky Mountain spotted fever, other kinds of tick-bite fevers (tick typhus), rabbit fever (tularemia), and tick paralysis.

 (2) Soft ticks transmit famine fever (tick-borne relapsing fever).

 (3) For individual protection, wear clothing impregnated with clothing repellent, and supply skin repellent to exposed areas. In a tick infested area, personnel should examine their bodies every 3-4 hours and remove any attached ticks. This can be facilitated, by using the "buddy-system." At semipermanent camps, brush and vegetation should be removed.

 c. Diseases Transmitted by Sand Flies (Phlebotomus Flies).

 (1) Sand-fly fever, 3-day fever (pappataci fever), oriental sore, Delhi boil, and tropical sores are sand-fly borne.

 (2) For individual protection, use insect repellent, aerosols, protective clothing, and mosquito bar. In semipermanent camps, clear area of rubbish, debris, and ruins. Apply

residual insecticide spray to inside of walls and around tent entrances.

 d. Diseases Transmitted by Fleas.

 (1) The rat flea is a carrier of Black Death (bubonic plague) and murine typhus. The fleas of other rodents may also transmit these diseases.

 (2) For individual protection, apply skin repellent to exposed parts of body and impregnate clothing with clothing repellent. In semipermanent camps apply residual insecticide spray or dust to floor and lower wall of tents, rodent burrows, and around rodent traps.

 e. Diseases Transmitted by Body Lice.

 (1) The body louse and head louse may transmit jail fever (epidemic typhus fever), and famine fever (relapsing fever).

 (2) For individual protection against body lice, apply insecticide powder over inner surface of underclothing and to seams on inside of outer clothing. For head lice apply louse powder freely to the area of head covered by hair.

 /.• Disease Transmitted by Mites.

 (1) Mites are widely distributed throughout the world. In the United States and Europe, the variety known as chiggers (red bugs) produce considerable skin irritation which may become secondarily infected from scratching. In the Far East, the six-legged larval stage of trombiculid mites transmit "scrub" typhus fever (Japanese river fever or tsutsugamushi fever).

 (2) For individual protection, apply skin repellent to exposed parts of the body and impregnate outer clothing and socks with clothing repellent. At semipermanent camps, clear camp sites of grass and other vegetation by burning or bulldozing.

 g. Diseases Transmitted by Bloodsucking Flies.

 (1) Deer flies (chrysops) transmit rabbit-fever (tularemia) and the filarial African eye-worm (loa-loa). In Central America black flies and buffalo gnats transmit a filarial worm (Onchocerca volvulus) which causes a troublesome filarial disease. The tsetse fly of Central Africa transmits sleeping sickness (trypanosomiasis).

 (2) Mosquito nets, protective clothing, insect repellent, and insecticide aerosols should be

used as preventive measures.

h. Diseases Transmitted by Triatomidae \'7bCone-nose Bugs, Assassin or Kissing Bugs). Cone-nose bugs may transmit American Trypanosomiasis (Chagas disease). To avoid these insects, do not sleep in native huts, native shops, stables, barns, and chicken houses. For individual protection, use mosquito nets and protective clothing. At semipermanent camps or stations, buildings should be screened.

i. Diseases Transmitted by Vampire Bats. Vampire bats transmit rabies (hydrophobia) to human beings and animals. The virus of rabies is carried in the saliva of the infected bat. Immediate first aid treatment consists of washing with soap and water, followed by an antiseptic and a sterile dressing. Antirabic treatment must be administered to persons bitten by this species of bat. Immediate first-aid

treatment consists of cauterizing the bite wound with trichloroacetic acid or nitric acid. After cauterization, the wound is treated by the application of sterile tannic acid ointment and a tight compression bandage.

100. Water Borne Diseases

a. Diseases. Typhoid fever, the paratyphoid fevers bacillary dysentery, amebiasis, cholera, and other diseases may be transmitted by infected water which is used for drinking and culinary purposes. Schistosomiasis (blood fluke) may readily be encountered in surface water while bathing or swimming, and through drinking. When the fluke is known to be present, water must be avoided. Standard methods of purifying water serve to destroy the larvae of the fluke, but it must be emphasizd that at least one part per million of chlorine must be present after a 30-minute contact period.

b. Preventive Measures.

(1) Sources. Water selected for human consumption should be the cleanest available. Ground water from wells, springs, and infiltration galleries is usually less contaminated, clearer, cooler, and generally more palatable. However, since ground water is limited in quantity, the most common source in the jungles will be surface supplies such as streams, ponds, and lakes. Care must be exercised in selecting the water point to insure that bathing, laundering, and vehicle washing is done downstream.

(2) Engineer water points. Whenever possible all drinking water should be procured from engineer water points. Minimum treatment should consist of the following steps: Prechlorination, chemical coagulation, settling, and filtration with postchlorination if the finished water contains less than the required one part per million chlorine residual. (3) Emergency and individual water disinfection.

(a) Lyster hag disinfection. Only the cleanest water available should be used. Suspended matter may be strained out through cloth or an improvised sand - filter. One glass tube of grade A calcium hypochlorite (QM Stock No! 51-W-125) dissolved in the 36-gallon bag provides a dosage of 2.5 p. p. m. After 10 minutes, the chlorine residual is measured with the orthotolidine kit provided with the tubes. If the chlorine measures less than 1.0 p. p. m., another tube is added to the contents of the bag.

(5) Canteen disinfection. Each man should be provided with an adequate supply of. individual water purification tablets (QM Stock No. 51-T-1498) for use on extended patrols or when otherwise isolated from his unit. Generally, adequate disinfection is obtained when one tablet is used for clear water and two tablets for cloudy or turbid water. Other methods such as boiling and the squad method of chlorinating canteens are discussed in detail in EM 21-10.

(4) Other water sources. Water may be obtained during heavy rainfall by catchment from roofs of tents and buildings. This water must then be disinfected before consumption. Sea water

can be distilled either in standard engineer equipment or in small quantities with an improvised distillation unit. Such facilities are bulky, extremely heavy, and require large amounts of fuel. Their use is justified only when fresh water is not available.

TOT. Intestinal Infections

a. Diseases. The principal diseases in this group which occur in the tropics are amoebic dysentery, bacillary (bacterial) dysentery, cholera, food infection, food intoxication, worms (helminthic infections), paratyphoid fevers, protozoal dysenteries, typhoid fever, and imdulant fever (Malta fever). These diseases are usually transmitted by eating or drinking contaminated food or water. Contamination of food is common. The contamination may be caused in vegetable products by contact with infected material during growth, such as human excreta used as a fertilizer. Contamination of any food may be caused by dirty utensils or by food handlers who have, or are carriers of, intestinal diseases. Native fruits and vegetables which cannot be peeled or cooked should not be eaten.

b. Preventive Measures.

(1) All perishables, both meats and vegetables, I which cannot be stored in a refrigerator below 40° F., should be cooked immediately upon receipt, except that frozen meat should

be cooked immediately after thawing. All nonperishable food should be stored in vermin-free boxes or chests. All food should be kept as free of dust as possible, and every effort must be made to prevent contamination during transit. (2) AH foods should be served immediately after preparation. No leftovers should be served. Hard bread, canned meat, and other canned foods should be issued to troops in position unless hot food can be brought up in original containers. Sandwiches and other food for lunches should not be prepared and issued for later consumption.

102. Special Tropical Diseases

Yaws (frambesia), tropical bubo (lymphogranuloma inguinale), and granuloma inguinale are diseases which may be transmitted through sexual intercourse. Tropical bubo is a virus disease. The initial lesion is so small that it usually passes unnoticed. Later the lymph glands in the groin become enlarged, break down, and ulcerate. Granuloma inguinale is usually limited to the genitalia and inguinal region, but may spread to other parts of the body. The lesions consist of large ulcerating areas which spread, gradually destroying the tissues as they advance.

103. Fungus Diseases of Skin and Hair

a. Diseases. Ringworm (tinea); athlete's foot (epidermophytosis of the feet) ; pinta, a disease of the skin characterized by whitish patches, and tri-chophytosisj a fungus disease of the hair, are the principal fungus diseases. The seriousness of these

diseases, especially those of the ears and feet, is seldon realized except by men with long jungle experience. These diseases are especially serious in the jungle because—

(1) The climate favors the growth of the microscopic plants called fungi which produce these diseases.

(2) Sweat soaked skin invites attack by fungus.

(3) More individual effort is required to keep the body and clothes clean.

(4) The extreme fatigue resulting from jungle marching is apt to cause soldiers to neglect to wash their clothes and bodies even though they have been told that their health depends on cleanliness.

(5) Some men lacking jungle experience falsely believe they are tough enough to stay healthy in the tropics and need not take the precautions prescribed.'

b. Preventive Measures. It is much easier to prevent fungus diseases of the skin and hair than to cure them. The following preventive measures are important:

(1) Keep as clean as possible, and wash as often as is practicable. Use plenty of soap and

water when available, both for bathing and washing clothes. Socks should be washed with soap at least once a day. If a stream cannot be reached after making camp, use a part of the water in the canteen and a little soap to wash at least the armpits, groin, and feet.

(2) Do not go barefooted in the jungle.

(3) As far as possible, avoid soiling clothes. Avoid mud. Use the machete to provide a clean place to rest during halts. Unnecessary dirtiness is a sign of stupidity, not toughness.

(4) Keep the skin dry, well ventilated, and free from tight clothing. Wear only enough clothing to afford protection from insects and thorns. Do not wear underclothes unless the outer clothing chafes you. Wear clothing and shoes that will allow air to reach the skin.

(5) Sleep with as little clothing as the temperature permits. Never sleep in wet, dirty clothing.

(6) When the tactical situation permits, sleep off the ground, preferably in a hammock or on a platform.

(7) Clean under and around the nails of the hands and feet.

(8) Take sun-baths for short periods whenever practicable, but do not let the skin burn.

(9) Stay away from native houses. Live and . camp in clean, uninhabited jungle.

(10) Dust socks and the insides of shoes with foot powder.

(11) Wash and sun articles, such as packboards, used by more than one man.

(12) Officers and NCO's must hold frequent foot inspections.

c. Individual Jungle Treatment of Fungus Shin Infections. - ' ; (1) During prolonged jungle operations, each soldier must take care of his skin and l mkke
, every possible effort to keep infected skin areas clean, dry, well-ventilated, and protected. Soap and water help to cure, as well as prevent, fungus infections.

(2) After washing and just before retiring, treat infected skin areas with antifungus medicine or half-strength iodine. Do not scratch insect bites. Iodine should not be applied before exercising or exposure to sunlight. In rashes around the crotch and under the arms use the army fungicidal ointment. The army foot powder helps both foot and body rashes of the milder types.

(3) In general, avoid bandages and greasy medicines. Dry up fungus infections with drying medicines in conjunction with air and sunlight.

(4) Clean off dead, infected skin. Do not scratch.

(5) Boil clothing, especially socks, when you have the opportunity. Do not wear one sock first on an infected foot and then on a healthy foot. Dry, stretch, and soften socks before replacing in field kit.

(6) Avoid overtreating. Follow instructions. Do not use too much medicine or apply it too often.

(7) Consider all skin diseases as serious. Treat them regularly, intelligently, and patiently.

d. Remedial Action. Fungus diseases, if neglected, will incapacitate many men, regardless of personal cleanliness and the use of foot powder. At the. first symptoms of a fungus infection, use the prescribed' medicine carried in the individual or group

first-aid kits. When inflammation or itching is excessive consult a medical officer as soon as possible.

104. Venomous Snakes and Snake-Bite Treatment

a. Venomous Snakes.

(1) Poisonous and nonpoisonous snakes may be expected in jungle areas wherever there are many small rodents, frogs, or other animals which are food for snakes. Although most of the Pacific islands are completely free of snakes, a check should be made with island natives or evacuating troops to ascertain whether snakes are to be found in occupied areas. Snakes exist on

all tropical mainlands.

(2) An important fact to remember about snakes is that more people are bitten while trying to catch or kill snakes than in any other way. 95 percent of all snakes are docile, are afraid of man, and will flee into hiding, or escape if given the opportunity. Exceptions to this are the cottonmouth water moccasin of the southern United States, the Fer-de-lance and Bushmaster of Central and South America, and the Taipan of northern Australia and New Guinea. There is no dependable rule by which a venomous snake can be distinguished from a harmless one at any considerable distance. If a snake is found, it should be tested with the same precaution as a high explosive "dud"; it should be left alone. In general, the most effective snake repellent is cleanliness. Open garbage pits, carelessly discarded ration con-tamers, or other types of carelessness which provide food for rats, mice, or other vermin also attract snakes which eat these small animals. Strict policing of occupied areas will discourage snakes, as well as noxious pests. b. Snake Bite.

(1) The bite of a, poisonous snake is accompanied by a sharp, burning pain which spreads rapidly. On examination, the wound will show one or two deep scratches or punctures where the fangs have pierced the skin. These wounds usually do not bleed profusely, but are very painful. The snake should be killed, if possible, and shown to a medical officer, since the type of antivenom used depends on the kind of snake involved. Even if the snake should be found to be nonpoison-ous, the bite should be treated medically, because the wound is multiple and dirty, and very likely to become infected.

(2) Having killed the snake, it may be identified generally as follows: Poisonous snakes have—

(a) Elliptical pupils in their eyes—like those of a cat.
(b) Large bodies and diamond- or spade-shaped heads.
(c) A single row of belly plates behind the vent.
(d) Prominent forward teeth or fangs, usually curved to the rear. Not all poisonous snakes conform to this description; the above points serve only as a general guide. If the lite is accompanied by a severe pain, the snake is poisonous. If no snake-bite kit is available, proceed promptly as follows, using whatever materials are at hand: Sit down. Apply a tourniquet between the bite and the heart and adjacent to the wound. Apply it tightly enough to prevent venous blood from returning to the heart, but loosely enough to permit arterial blood to circulate. A rope, belt, necktie, undershirt, shirt sleeve, or communication wire may be used as a field expedient tourniquet. Using a knife, razor, or other sharp cutting edge, make crisscross incisions across the fang marks and on any swollen or discolored areas. These incisions should be about one-quarter inch across and as deep as the fangs are believed to have penetrated. Twist the tourniquet so that a flow of blood comes from the wound, and start suction on the incisions. If possible the patient should do the sucking, but if he is unable to reach the area of the bite, another person should carry out the procedure. If the inside of the mouth is intact, it is safe to suck the blood and poison out of the wounds and spit it out. If there are open sores or bad teeth in the mouth, there is a risk of mild illness from the poison, but this risk is minimal compared to the danger confronting the person who has been bitten by the snake. After applying first-aid, ride (if possible) or walk slowly to an aid station for medical treatment. The tourniquet should be kept in place until medical attention is gained. Remember to take the dead snake to the aid station for identification. The snake-bite suction kit consists of a tourniquet, iodine applicator, lancet, mechanical suction pump, ammonia inhalant, and adhesive compresses, in a plastic carrying case. The tourniquet is applied immediately, between the wound and the heart, and close to the wound. It is tight enough to restrict venous blood from returning to the

heart, but permit arterial blood to enter the injured area. The wounds are then painted with iodine, and the lancet is used to make cross-incisions as deep as the fang punctures, and long enough to assure free bleeding. The suction applicator is applied, filling the applicator with blood, venom, and air, and the extracted matter being expelled on the ground. This suction process continues for one hour. Sterile dressings are placed over the wound (s) and the individual being treated is evacuated to a medical officer for further treatment. The tourniquet remains in place during the entire operation. Venom can be extracted from the tissues as late as three to five hours after the bite. Multiple crisscross incisions should be. made over the swollen area, especially at the advancing edge of the swelling, and suction applied. After applying the first aid, move the patient to an aid station for medical treatment.

(5) Do not attempt "home remedies" such as drinking alcohol, cauterizing the wound, eating the snake, or using potassium permanganate—they do not work, and they are very dangerous. Immediate suction followed by antivenom injections are the best treatment, and the sooner they are applied, the quicker will be the recovery.

Section III. EVACUATION

105. General

The usual equipment and property prescribed by the table of organization and equipment for units concerned with evacuation are not always suitable for operations under jungle conditions. Standard cross-country ambulances are seldom practicable on jungle trails, in swamps, and on unimproved muddy roads, rutted by heavy traffic. For this reason, other types of vehicles, particularly weapons carriers and %-ton trucks, may be used for transporting the wounded. All types of transportation, whether by water, land, or air may be used to transport casualties to the rear. This principle applies not only to vehicles assigned primarily for this purpose, but also to empty supply vehicles returning from forward positions. Evacuation in the jungle should normally be along supply routes which are adequately protected against enemy action. Boats, rafts, and ambulance barges may be used for short distances when practicable to evacuate by water. When open terrain or water permits landings and takeoff, fixed-wing aircraft and helicopters provide an excellent and rapid means of evacuation.

106. Litters

The standard folding litter has some disadvantages when evacuation involves the crossing of streams, gullies, and steep slopes. Metal basket litters (Stokes) are more practicable under these conditions and can also be used to advantage when casualties are being moved from jungle areas to ships for evacuation by water. The metal basket litter can be used with the cacolet type pack saddle to evacuate casualties by pack animal. Native litter bearers may prefer to use ordinary canvas sheets with loops for poles. The canvas sheeting is light, and poles may be cut when needed. All available means for collecting and transporting the sick and wounded must be used to do the job satisfactorily. Ordinarily, no one method will suffice. For general methods of transporting the sick and wounded, see FM 8-35.

107. Human Factors

a. It is easy to overestimate the strength and endurance of litter squads. Well-conditioned men, carrying a patient on a litter for 400 to 600 yards over jungle terrain, are unable to repeat the performance without an appreciable amount of rest. Surgeons must keep their commanders informed of the adequacy and efficiency of the evacuation system, and commanders must provide additional natives when practicable and, at times, men from other units of the command.

h. No man should be evacuated who may be treated locally and returned to duty.

CHAPTER 6 UNIT AND INDIVIDUAL TRAINING

Section I. GENERAL

108. Training Objectives

a. The first objective of jungle training is to get the individual used to the climate and to get him into the proper physical and mental condition to endure the rigors of jungle warfare.

b. The second objective is to train units in the technique of jungle operation. The tactics of jungle operations are the same as for any other terrain but, due to reduced visibility and limited communications, unit control presents many problems not common to open terrain.

109. Training Methods

Training is progressive and the training day is based on the prevailing climate. Training is generally divided into three phases.

a. The first phase is on a reduced schedule. It is based on the amount of service the troops have previously had in this type of climate. The program includes physical training consisting largely of marches through jungle terrain, combined with formal physical training as outlined in FM 21-20 and acclimatization as covered in appropriate official publications. ■ The men are taught the rudiments

no

of survival, and the basic techniques of jungle navigation, and are given a thorough course in individual sanitation and hygiene. . Commanders must impress on their men the necessity for hygiene and sanitation throughout all operations in the jungle.

The second phase of training includes advanced individual training in survival and jungle navigation, and an increase in the time devoted to physical training. During this period, practical application of the techniques of survival and navigation are combined with physical training in the form of extended maneuvers covering distances up to 20 miles and for periods of from 2 to 3 days duration.

c. The third phase of training is devoted entirely to unit and combined arms training. . It includes company problems over long distances and against an active aggressor force. The technique of sound adjustment of mortar and artillery fires must be stressed. The offensive phase stresses movement through the jungle both on and off trails, resupply, stealth, and navigation. Units should spend from 7 to 14 days in actual operations under jungle conditions without returning to a base camp. Combined exercises emphasizing the control and coordination between the supporting arms and the maneuvering infantry must be conducted.

d. During all phases of training it should be impressed on the men that the jungle, if properly used, is an ally, both in the offense and defense. The commander takes every opportunity to improve the aggressive spirit of the unit and to show by example and by practical application that troops can live and fight and win in jungle terrain.

110. Psychological Adjustment

a. The jungle is a strange experience to the man who is unfamiliar with this type terrain. To overcome instinctive fears and uncertainties, commanders must condition the soldier's mind for this new experience. The men must be given confidence in their ability to live, move, and operate in a jungle. This training begins with physical training which increases a man's physical ability and makes him sure that he can do whatever is required, regardless of the physical hardship. The soldier must be thoroughly indoctrinated in techniques of survival. He must be confident of his ability to exist alone and find his way to safety if he becomes separated from his unit. He must know that he can survive over a considerable period of time on jungle vegetation without conventional rations. He must be sure of his ability to cope with the wild life of the jungle.

b. One of the greatest causes of low morale among troops serving in the jungle is inactivity. Commanders must make every effort to keep their men busy, particularly during the training period and just before entering combat.

Section II. PRACTICAL HINTS FOR JUNGLE LIVING

111. Care of Weapons, Clothing, and Equipment

a. Weapons, clothing, and equipment receive hard usage in the jungle. Men must be trained to protect all articles and to clean, dry, or repair them whenever practicable. Our weapons and equipment are the best and will not become unserviceable unless neglected, but the damp heat of the jungle areas requires that special care be given to all equipment in daily or frequent use. The humidity, mud, and the frequent shortage of oil and other materials necessary for cleaning weapons combine to make weapon maintenance in the jungle particularly difficult. All weapons and equipment must receive constant preventive maintenance. The potential battle efficiency of a combat unit undergoing training can be determined almost precisely by the condition in which it maintains weapons and equipment. Equally, this reflects the military leadership qualities of its officers and noncommissioned officers.

b. One of the most important duties of subordinate leaders is to carry out frequent personal inspections to determine the state of maintenance of weapons, ammunition, magazines, spare parts, and accessories. Time and circumstances will rarely permit a thorough inspection of all weapons in a platoon at one time. Under such circumstances, frequent random inspections or spot checks will be made.

(1) All personnel (including officers) of a unit operating in the jungle should carry individual small cans of preservative lubricating oil. Extra oil must be carried by members of machine-gun squads.

(2) In hot, humid climates, light or special preservative lubricating oil should be used on weapons. In salt-water atmosphere, medium preservative lubricating oil should be used.

(3) Three or four cleaning rods must be carried in each rifle squad. Patches should be carried by each individual.

(4) Weapons must be disassembled, inspected, and cleaned daily. In rainy weather, it may be necessary to do this two or three times a day. By laying rifles on crotched sticks several inches off the ground and placing large (e. g., banana, palm fronds, etc.) leaves over them, they can be kept dry.

(5) Breech mechanisms can be protected by tying an oil-soaked cloth around them. This should be attached in such a manner that the cloth can be easily removed by means of a quick pull on one end.

(6) Wooden parts of weapons should be inspected to see that swelling caused by moisture does not cause binding of the working parts. If swelling occurs, shave off only enough wood to relieve the binding. A light coat of raw linseed oil applied at intervals and well rubbed in with the heel of the hand will help to keep out moisture. Allow oil to soak in for a few hours and then wipe and polish the wood with a dry clean rag. Care should be taken to see that linseed oil does not get into the mechanism as it will gum up when dry. The stock and hand guard should be dismounted when this oil is applied.

(7) Accessories, spare parts, and magazines will rust and deteriorate rapidly if not cared for diligently.

(8) Optical equipment such as mortar sights, compasses, and field glasses, when not in use, should receive special care and should be protected from moisture to prevent fungus.

(9) All machetes must be sharpened and oiled before going into a jungle operation. One man in the squad should carry a small whetstone for sharpening machete blades which soon get badly dulled and nicked.

(10) Tropical insects, especially termites and ants, often damage or destroy fabrics or wood in a few hours. Therefore, when practicable, clothing and equipment should be hung off the ground away from most of the destructive insects. Troop leaders should check to see that their men hang their clothing, packs, shoes, etc., from bushes, ropes, or other available supports.

(11) Exposing clothing and equipment to sunlight to dry and kill germs is desirable. However, unnecessary exposure of fabrics to intense tropical sunlight deteriorates them and bleaches even the best of dyes.

c. A tendency exists to turn in dirty clothing and to draw clean clothes when possible rather than to launder them. When the situation is active, this is to be expected as no time exists for washing clothes. When the situation is stabilized, dirty clothes should be boiled and washed. Enforcement of these provisions is a function of command.

d. Immediate disciplinary action must be taken when men waste or lose their equipment through carelessness. Much equipment will be unavoidably lost or damaged incident to training and active operations. Such losses are legitimate, but wastage due to carelessness is a serious military offense.

112. Machete

a. Of prime importance in the discussion of equipment required for jungle operations is the use and maintenance of the machete. From the standpoint of the individual soldier, this item, perhaps more than any single item, is the distinctive property of the jungle fighter. A machete is the most effective tool for cutting through the jungle. The machete is an effective weapon for attacking at night when silence is imperative and for defense against attack when firing, reloading weapons, or throwing hand grenades is impracticable.

b. The machete is a cutting instrument that depends on velocity rather than weight for its effectiveness. Maximum velocity and resulting efficiency are obtained by slashing with plenty of whip in the blade. The starting position for a blow with a machete is to hold the handle tightly with the thumb and first two fingers. The blade should be turned backwards toward the-forearm. When striking, the fingers and wrist should snap the machete forward, using plenty of wrist and finger movement and not by swinging with the whole arm and shoulder. The blade of the machete should strike an object at an angle of about $45°$. Proficiency in handling a machete is obtained by practical work in cutting brush and making trails.

c. When a patrol is cutting across jungle on a compass course, men should be placed in the following order: First, the leading machete man cuts as fast as he is able to in the direction indicated by the group, leader. Next, one or two other machete men open up the trail so those following do not have to force their way. The patrol leader should place himself in the third or fourth position from the column. He should guide the leading machete man on a carefully selected compass course. The patrol leader should indicate the correct course to the leading machete man, either by pointing or by quietly telling him the number of degrees he should move to the right or left. There should always be five or more yards between adjacent men, whether in movement or at a halt. Since heat prostration is one of the most common causes of casualties during hard jungle marches, leaders should give their men a five-minute rest every 30 or 40 minutes. The leading machete man works the hardest; therefore, he should be replaced every 15 or 20 minutes.

  d. A neAvly issued machete has a rather dull thick edge. After being sharpened, this edge is suitable for cutting hard wood and for clearing land where there is likelihood of striking rocks that Avould damage a thin ground blade. For cutting across tropical jungle, however, a machete blade should have a thin, tapered knife edge and should come to a gradual point. The blade should be sharpened as soon as possible after issue on a whetstone or a water-cooled natural-stone grindstone that will not overheat the steel. To use and take care of the machete—

  (1) Sharpen it whenever practicable.

  (2) Oil it to prevent rusting. A thick vaseline or grease is best.

  (3) Leave the handle as issued. Do not notch the handle or wrap it with tape or cord. Koughness will blister the hand.

  (4) Do not use the free hand to grasp a vine or limb that is being cut.

304492°—54 8

  (5) Avoid striking the blade in the ground. Striking a stone will damage the thin cutting edge of a well-sharpened machete.

  (6) Sheath the machete when not in use.

  (7) When carrying a naked machete, turn the edge away from the legs and body.

  (8) Never cut directly downward toward the feet. Slant all blows to right or left.

  (9) Be sure that no one is within swinging distance of a machete in use. Keep a safe distance from other men using machetes.

  113. Sleeping

  a. During the rainy season, a man must sleep off the ground and under a mosquito net. He should have an insect-proof hammock that is made of light, durable, waterproof material. The hammock should have a rainproof, adjustable tojo with attachable insect netting, and should not exceed 6 joounds in weight complete with netting. In dry weather, a man can sleep comfortably on the ground in a sleejo-ing bag improvised from ponchos. In scrub typhus country, if sleeping on the ground cannot be avoided, a blanket, poncho, or shelter half well dusted with insect repellent should be j^laced between the ground and the man.

  b. Lacking a hammock like the one described above, improvised hammocks or jungle beds may be used. Hammocks may be made of blankets, pieces of canvas, or shelter halves. A two-man, otf-the-ground jungle bed may be made as follows: Plant four forked posts firmly in the ground with the forks 1 foot above the ground. Lay a frame of 2-inch poles in the forks and fill in this frame by laying thinner

poles across it. Fasten the poles together with vines or strips of bark. Cover this platform with light branches and leaves to form a mattress. Be sure that the branches and leaves used for this purpose are free of insects. Spread a blanket over this mattress to hold everything in place, and pitch the shelter tent and mosquito net over it. In dry weather, the mosquito net (without the shelter tent) is the only cover needed.

  114. Food

  a. Food for jungle service should be selected to give maximum food value with a minimum weight. Cooking utensils are hard to keep free of bacteria, and cooked food can become contaminated while being delivered to the troops. Foods should be limited to those which are ready to eat with little or no cooking. When cooking is necessary, each man or group of men should do their own cooking and should eat the cooked food at once.

  i. All packaged rations may be eaten unheated. The assault ration may be used as an individual reserve or emergency ration. Canned fruit juice may be issued to supplement the basic rations. Only the beverage component needs to be prepared in any way.

c. All soldiers should learn to cook rice, a staple of most oriental diets which will usually be contained in the captured rations of oriental ■ armies operating in a jungle.

d. Waterproof food bags are designed to carry dry rations under humid conditions. These bags are made of high-grade coated materials and should be retained for reuse. Ration containers protect their
contents from insects and from contact with humid air. However, this protection ends (even for dry foods such as milk powder and dried fruits) as soon as the containers are broken or opened. All wet or damp foods must be eaten immediately after opening the containers. Dry foods may be kept for several days, provided they are placed at once in waterproof food bags, and the bags are securely closed.

e. Clean food is essential to the health of a command. The following are basic rules for keeping food clean.

(1) Keep flies, rats, and all insects away from food and utensils.

(2) Stay away from native buildings.

(3) Wash the hands before eating. The use of soap is essential if cleanliness is to be assured.

(4) Disinfect each drinking or eating utensil. Scalding, or dipping in a chlorine solution will kill germs.

(5) If it is necessary to eat food cooked by natives, be sure to eat it as soon as its is prepared and while it is very hot. Place it in utensils which have been washed agid disinfected.

(6) Clean the top of every can and the can opener by pouring a small amount of boiling water over them, or by using disinfected water from the canteen.

(7) Cook all meats until they are thoroughly done.

(8) Cook only enough food for one meal. Do not keep cooked food for future meals.

(9) Eemove the skin of any fruit before eating. Do not bite through the skin.

115. Cooking Utensils

a. Most cooking in the jungle is done by individuals or small groups of men who pool their resources and prepare food for themselves in one or two containers. Generally, the only cooking utensils available are empty ration cans, canteen cups, or the soldiers' mess kits.

b. Cooking utensils need include only a spoon and a metal container for boiling. The canteen cup is useful both as a cooking and eating utensil. Most foods obtained in the jungle can be cooked over an open fire.

c. Where bamboo is available, a section of green stem cut below two successive joints will furnish a container closed at the bottom and open at the top. This will make a suitable vessel for improvised cooking. Green bamboo is so durable that water may be boiled in it.

d. A coral stone or porous lava stone is very useful for grating foods. A splinter of bamboo makes a sharp knife for cutting food.

e. Almost any food may be roasted merely by placing it in hot embers or broiled by holding it on a stick over a hot fire.

/. A ground oven is easy to make. Simply scrape out a shallow pit in the earth or sand, lay down kindling .and some larger firewood, and lay stones on top of the firewood and set the kindling afire. When the stones have been heated as much as possible, place the food wrapped in green leaves on them; then cover with leaves or coconut "cloth" and finally
with earth or sand; the food should be ready for eating within an hour. Food left in a ground oven until eaten is safe from ants, flies, and other small pests.

116. Medical Care

The soldier must provide his own first aid by attending to his own scratches and bites at once. If medicines are in sealed kits or are carried inside a pack, men will not use them early or often enough for preventive purposes. Each man should carry, easily available, a small bottle of antiseptic and a small roll of adhesive tape. Water purification tablets, salt (sodium chloride) tablets, chloroquine, and a small bottle of insect repellent should be carried by each man. A supply of these items is included in the individual first-aid kit.

117. Expedients

Jungle expedients require both originality and forethought. The following suggestions will aid in the development of expedients by individuals and patrol leaders:

a. Carry matches in a waterproof container, or carry water-proofed matches; otherwise, perspiration alone will often make them useless.

b. Never go anywhere without a compass, preferably a lensatic or prismatic compass, and know how to use it.

c. Carry a light hook and line or a light gig, such as a spear with barbed points, for fishing. Stunning fish with a stick of black powder or other explosive is the quickest and surest way of getting a good catch.

d. Next to the machete, a. good knife is a man's most useful possession in the jungle.

e. Ponchos, in addition to their primary use as raincoats, may be made into improvised sleeping-bags, sun shelters, and tents.

/. A watch is useful in determining direction and approximating distances.

g. Most mud or other solids in water can be removed by straining the water through a cloth. Stirring a small amount of alum into the water causes the solids to settle. If used for drinking, the water must then be boiled or otherwise disinfected.

. h, If lost, remember that if a man goes down slope he will come to a stream, and that watercourses, besides furnishing a means of travel and a supply of water and food, always lead to inhabited valleys or coastal regions.

%. Do not attempt to travel alone at night. Halt early enough to make camp, build a fire, and collect plenty of firewood before darkness.

j. To build a fire in wet weather, first select a spot for it that is sheltered from the rain. Split out the heartwood of dead limbs broken from trees to start the fire. A small can of solidified alcohol is useful for starting a fire if damp wood must be used for fuel. The can of alcohol will last for many days. The synthetic fire tablet may be used, if available.

k. Vines can be used in place of string or rope for many purposes.

I. Edible fruits can usually be identified by signs of animals having eaten them. Do not eat unknown fruits and plants as some of them contain deadly poisons.

m. Sleep off the ground to avoid dampness, reptiles, and insects. Climb a tree if mosquitoes and ether insects are bad near the ground.

n. If possible, travel with one or more companions.

o. Do not fear the jungle. A man can travel alone for weeks in uninhabited country if he does not become panicky. Do not try to tear a path through-vines of other jungle growth. Cutting a path saves energy. Pick a route carefully, making full use of the sun, the stars, the compass, and the terrain to maintain direction.

p. Know how to find water. Small amounts can be found in certain plants, including the wild grapes, the traveller's palm, and the water vine. Coral will grow in salt water only, so sand breaks in a coral reef often indicate that fresh water may be found several feet below the surface.

118. Dealing With the Natives

a. Native inhabitants of jungle areas can be of valuable assistance to military forces if their attitude is friendly and their cooperation is cultivated. Until the sentiments of native inhabitants have been determined, they must be regarded with suspicion. A commander should take early measures to ascertain the sentiment of natives. Once their friendly attitude is established, he should attempt to avail himself of their assistance to whatever extent possible.

b. Friendly natives have been employed as scouts or guides, carrier, litter bearers, and as laborers. Friendly inhabitants are also valuable sources of military intelligence. In some cases, natives niay form their own fighting groups. These forces, though perhaps limited in military experience, have the advantages of a detailed knowledge of the terrain and may be useful for scouting, raiding, and harassing enemy-communications. The use of native troops, organized and controlled by the commander, will not only help to lessen objection to the presence of our forces but will strengthen solidarity against a common enemy.

c. In the employment of native inhabitants, several limitations will be encountered. Native languages vary widely. Local interpreters are usually available and sometimes "pidgin English" or sign language are acceptable measures for minimizing the language barrier. Some natives may be experienced fighters but probably are bewildered by the weapons of modern war. For this reason, reports by natives concerning the size, armament, formation, and equipment of the enemy must be carefully evaluated and verified when possible.

d. Wherever possible, dealings with the natives should be through a proper agent, such as a colonial administrator or head man of the district. Agreements relative to employment, pay, and rewards should be made through the designated agent. This agent should be carefully consulted as to native religions, superstitions, and customs; their local rules and customs should be meticulously respected. Natives should be paid a fair price for everything purchased from them in accordance with the medium of exchange of the locality. Individuals should not be permitted to barter or trade with the natives except with the approval of the agent.

e. In summary, since operations may be materially affected by the attitude of natives, their friendship and cooperation must be cultivated. A jungle soldier who abuses or antagonizes the natives is working against himself. A jungle soldier must never use terrorist methods against the natives. If a native is wronged, he becomes the enemy of the soldier who wronged him, and usually the enemy of our forces as a whole.

CD Z
z
<
bo .a '> ■
a 2
o cd
g 5
■a ^a
a 'co
en cd
CD -H
o 60
o ~"
.a
'C cd

APPENDIX REFERENCES

AR 220-50 Regiments—General Provisions. "
AR 220-60 Battalions—General Provisions.
AR 220-70 Companies—General Provisions.
FM 6-20 Artillery Tactics and Technique.
FM 6-101 The Field Artillery Battalion.
FM 7-10 Rifle Company, Infantry Regiment.
FM 7-20 Infantry Battalion.
FM 7-24 Communication in Infantry and Airborne Divisions.
FM 7-30 Service and Medical Companies, Infantry Regiment.
FM 7-35 Tank Company, Infantry Regiment.
FM 7-40 Infantry Regiment.
FM 17-32 Tank Platoon and Tank Company.
FM 17-33 Tank Battalion.
FM 21-5 Military Training.
FM 21-8 Military Training Aids.
FM 21-10 Military'Sanitation.
FM 21-11 First Aid for Soldiers.
FM 21-20 Physical Training.
FM 21-25 Elementary Map and Aerial Photograph Reading.
FM 21-30 Military Symbols.
FM 21-40 Defense Against Chemical Attack.
FM 21-45 Defense Against Biological Warfare.
FM 21-75 Combat Training of the Individual Soldier, and Patrolling.
FM 31-35 Air-Ground Operations. FM 44-2 Antiaircraft Ai'tillei-y Automatic Weapons.

FM 44-4 Antiaircraft Artillery Guns.

FM 101-5 Staff Organization and Procedure. SE 110-1-1 Index of Army Motion Pictures and Film Strips.

SK 320-5-1 Dictionary of United States Army Terms.

SK 320-50-1 Authorized Abbreviations.

Paragraph Page

Aircraft I 24 24

Communication 34 37

Air support, close 73-75 73

Ambushes:

Defense against 44 • 49

Offensive 37 41

Approach march 28 32

Artillery 52-62 61

Ammunition 59 63

Antiaircraft 62 65

Observation 56 62

Positions i 55 62

Targets 58 63

Assault 32 34

Attack:

Against hastily organized positions 35 39

Against prepared defenses 33 35

Assault 32 34

Conduct 31 33

Direction 31 33

Fire support 31, 33 33, 35

Night 36 40

Orders 30 33

Battalion medical platoon 92 90

Bivouac:

Security 25 27

Site 25' 27

Bunkers, destruction 33 35

CBR Warfare 76-81 74

Effectiveness 77, 78 75, 76

Smoke 78 76

Chlorination (water) 100 97

Paragraph Page

Command 7 10

Decentralized 2,26 3,31

Communication. 12, 82-88 13, 80

Aircraft 85 82

Equipment maintenance 82 80

(in) Metting engagements 34 37

Messenger 85 82

Pigeons 85 82
Radio 84 82
Sound 86 83
Visual 87 83
Wire 83 81
Control 2, 19 3, 17
Defense:
Camouflage 40 46
Conduct 42 48
Counterattack 43 49
Ground organization 40 46
Security 41 47
Terrain influence 39 45
Delaying movement ■ 46 50
Direction and control 2 3
Disease carriers 99 93
Diseases 98, 99, 101 92, 93, 99
Fungus 103 100
Intestinal 101 99
Preventive measures 99, 100, 103 93, 97, 100
Tropical 102 100
Waterfeorne 100 97
Division medical battalion 95 91
Engineers • 67-72 69
Bridge construction 68 70
Heavy equipment 72 72
Mapping 71 71
Minelaying 70 71
Road construction 67 69
Evacuation of casualties _■_ 96,105-107 91,108
Paragraph Page
First aid 116 122
Fleas : 99 93
Flies 99 93
Food 114, 117 119, 122
Cocking 114, 115 119, 121
Sanitation 114 119
Fungus diseases 103 100
Ground, organization 40 46
Halazone tablets 100 97
Halts:
Day 24 24
Night_: 24 24
Security 24 24
Helicopters 18, 24, 103 15, 24

Hygiene, personal 97 91
Hypochlorite ampoules 100 97
Inland waterways , 89c 86
Intestinal diseases 161 99
Iodine tablets • 100 97
Lice 99 93
Machine guns 50 58
Maps 20, 24 21, 24
March discipline 19 17
March objectives 21 22
Medical company headquarters 94 91
Medical service 91-96,116,117 89,122
Battalion medical platoon 92 90
Division medical battalion 95 91
Medical company headquarters 94 91
Regimental collecting platoon 93 90
Regimental medical company.j 91 89
Meeting engagement 34 37
Messengers 85 82
Mines (in defense) 46 50
Mites 99 93
Mortars.. 49 56
(in) Meeting engagements 34 37
Paragraph Pag e
Mosquitoes 99 93
Movement 14-17 14
Discipline 19 17
Night 22 22
Rate of march: lg 15
To contact 27 31
Naval gunfire employment 63 67
Navigation in jungles 24 24
Night halts . 24 24
Night marches 22 22
Observation 11 13
Orders, attack 30 33
Organization, unit 6 9
Patrols 38 43
Equipment 38 43
Overnight halts 38 43
Size of 38 43
Pill boxes, destruction 33 35
Preparatory fires 49 56
Radio communication 84 82
Rate of march 18 15
Reconnaissance 29, 33 32, 35

(in) Defense 39 45
Regimental Collection platoon 93 90
Regimental medical company 91 89
Reserves 34 37
Route selection 20 21
Sand flies 99 93
Sanitation 114 119
Security 23 23
Bivouac 25 27
Defense 41 47
Flank 16, 28 15, 32
Sleeping equipment 113 118
Smoke:
Signalling 78 76
Target marking 78 76
Snake-bite treatment 104 104
Paragraph Page
Snakes, venemous 104 104
Standing operating procedure 10 12
Supply:
Advance planning for 88 85
Animals 18,89 15,86
Classes 90 87
Deterioration 90 87
Difficulty 88, 90 85, 87
Hand carry 17 15
(by) Helicopter 89 86
Waterborne 89 86
Supporting weapons 47 53
Artillery 52-61 61
Machine guns 50 58
Mortars 49 56
Recoilless rifles 51 59
Tank (company) 48 54
Employment 64-66 67
Terrain features 3, 5 4, 7
Terrain in defense 39 45
Ticks 99 93
Training methods 109 110
Training, unit and individual 108-119 110
Transportation 13, 20 14, 21
Unit organization 6 9
Vegetation:
Cultivated areas 3 4
Grass 3 4
Influence in defense 39 45
Mangrove 3 4

Primary growth 3 4
Secondary growth 3 4
Rain forest 3 4
Visual communication 87 83
Weather 4 7
Wire communication 19, 83 17, 81
Withdrawal 46 50

[AG 353 (2 Jmi 54)]

By order of the Secretary of the Army:

M. B. KIDGWAY,
General, United States Army. Official: Chief of Staff.
JOHN A. KLEIN, Major General, United States Army, The Adjutant General.

Distribution: Active Army:
NG: Same as Active Army except allowance is one copy for each unit.
USAR: Same as Active Army except allowance is one copy for each unit.
Unless otherwise noted, distribution applies to ConUS and overseas.
For explanation of abbreviations used, see SR 320-50-1

U. S. GOVERNMENT PRINTING OFFICE; i9S4